George Dunlop Leslie

Riverside Letters

A Continuation of Letters to Macro

George Dunlop Leslie

Riverside Letters
A Continuation of Letters to Macro

ISBN/EAN: 9783744716550

Printed in Europe, USA, Canada, Australia, Japan

Cover: Foto ©Andreas Hilbeck / pixelio.de

More available books at **www.hansebooks.com**

RIVERSIDE LETTERS

A CONTINUATION OF
"LETTERS TO MARCO"

BY
GEORGE D. LESLIE, R.A.
AUTHOR OF "OUR RIVER"

WITH ILLUSTRATIONS BY THE AUTHOR

London
MACMILLAN AND CO., LTD.
NEW YORK: MACMILLAN & CO.
1896

To Marian

PREFACE

ENCOURAGED by the favourable reception that
my " Letters to Marco " met with, I continued,
during the last two years, to write to my old
friend.   Though the present letters were all
duly transmitted to Mr. Marks at the time
they were written, I cannot, as in the case
of the former series, say that I had no
thought of their afterwards appearing in
print.   For the sake of distinction I have
entitled them " Riverside Letters."

In these letters my readers will find many
notes and observations on my garden and
the plants and flowers in it, as to which I
felt that I had not said all I could have
wished in the former series.   Numerous as
are the books, by various writers, that have
recently appeared on Gardens and Flowers,

the subject is as inexhaustible as it is interesting, and it seems to me to be regretted that, considering how much admiration members of my profession have for flowers, so few of them have written anything on the subject.

I am sorry to say that, besides my own, I believe no artist's name appears on the list of Fellows of the Royal Horticultural Society. It would, I am convinced, greatly benefit the Society if a number of artists joined it as Fellows, and one or two of them were called upon annually to assist in judging the plants and awarding the prizes.

I take this opportunity of sincerely thanking all those kind friends 'who have helped to add interest to these letters by allowing me to make use of their instructive communications.

RIVERSIDE, WALLINGFORD, 1896.

CONTENTS

CONTENTS

ILLUSTRATIONS

FULL PAGE

IN THE TEXT

LETTER I

19th January, 1894.

DEAR MARCO—The following extract from a letter that I have received from Mr. E. G. Baker, of the Royal Gardens, Kew, on the subject of the blossom of the fig may be interesting to you, so I send it together with his drawing.

"——You say that you have been unable to find the flowers. As I happened to have by me a book giving a fair representation I thought, perhaps, it might interest you if I made a rough copy. The fig is the recep-

B

tacle, the flowers being inside. You perhaps
know the Dorstenia, which is commonly
grown in greenhouses, it is allied to the fig,
but here the receptacle is flat and the flowers
can be seen, while in the fig they are quite
hidden from view."

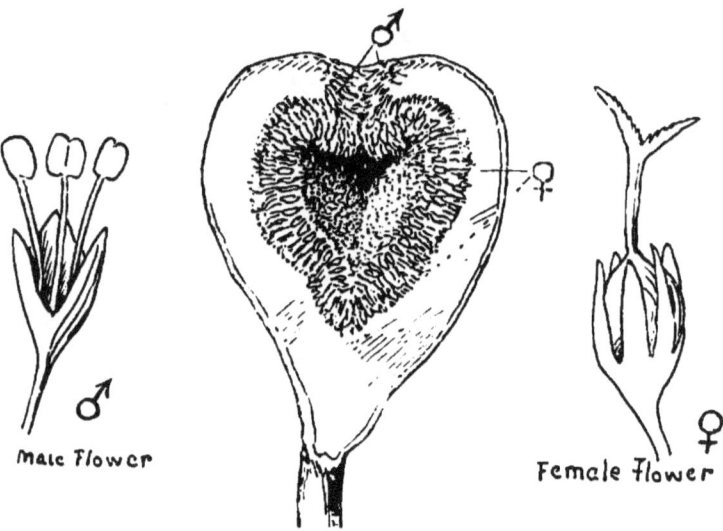

Male Flower   Female Flower

The little drawing that Mr. Baker sent me
explains the arrangement perfectly—the male
flowers being situated by themselves in the
little entrance to the interior of the fig, whilst
the females occupy the whole of the cavity

itself. The female flowers are shut up thus in a sort of harem, all together, the entrance to which is guarded by the males.

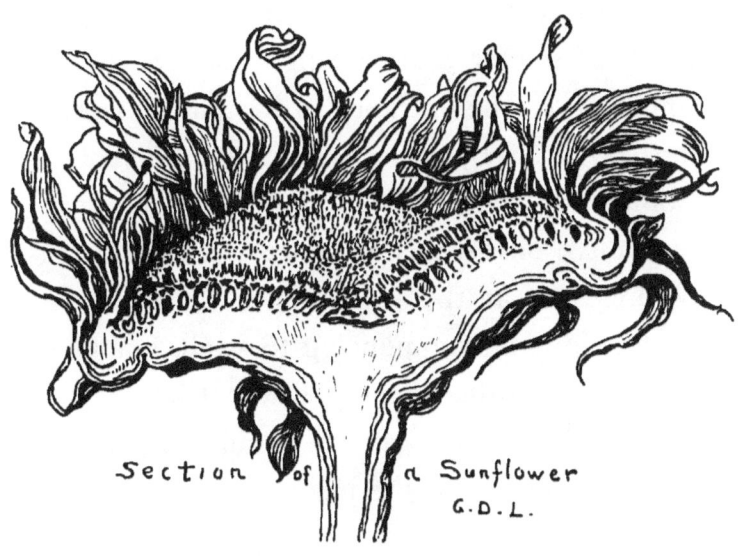

Section of a Sunflower
G.D.L.

I have not the opportunity of meeting a Dorstenia here, but I have cut a huge sunflower in half and drawn it as it partakes of a similar arrangement, for if you could close up this sunflower on to its centre something very like a fig would result. Anyhow it cannot be the *colour* or *beauty* of the flower that assists the fertilisation of the fig. I must, in justice to the evolutionists, however, state that in warm countries there is a very minute long-shaped insect that does make its way into the inside of the fig, and that fig culturers some-times pierce the entrance to hasten the ripen-ing, possibly by thus admitting the insect. Sometimes they also put one drop of very pure olive oil on this entrance. This has to be done just at the exact time when the fig shows signs of commencing to swell, but how this assists in the ripening I do not know, and it seems to me that the oil would effectually bar the entrance to the insect.

You will no doubt be as much pleased as I was by a bird anecdote sent to me by the Bishop of Reading; he writes :—" Perhaps the following may interest you, testifying as it does to a certainly remarkable exhibition of the sympathy between the human family and the birds. I have a friend, a small man, whose smallness was somewhat compensated by the possession of a luxuriant beard. At

the Winchester Quingentenary Celebration
this year I met him, reduced in size, and, like
Bottom, translated. The beard was gone.
The history of its disappearance was this.
In the spring of this year my friend—a most
ardent naturalist—watched from his dress-
ing-room window the nest-building of some
tits; they were sorely put to it for hair to
line the nest. How they made known to
him their want I know not, but the emergency
was so great, and their anxiety to be ready for
the coming family so urgent, that at last he
made up his mind to the sacrifice of his beard,
depositing the shorn glories on his window-
sill, and watching the process of weaving
the lining of the nest with calm regret and
satisfied charity."

LETTER II

12th February, 1894.

DEAR MARCO—I think I may congratulate
myself on the kind and favourable character
of the notices that my letters received in the
papers and reviews. Through the courtesy
of my publishers, I believe I must have seen
all that appeared, and I am glad to say
there were only two which were in any sense
adverse. The writers of these hostile notices
fell foul of the superficiality of my knowledge of natural history, both pointing out as
an example of this superficiality, the blunder I

made in the twenty-second letter as to the
gulls which my wife and I saw feeding with
the rooks on the flooded meadows opposite our
house.   I wrote : " They were probably the
small black-headed gull, *which at this time oj
the year lose their black caps;* at any rate,
these had white heads."   The words in italics
constitute my blunder.   I knew that a change
took place in the colour of the head at that
season, but had reversed, in my mind, the
order of the change at the time I wrote ; the
fact being that the birds in the spring change
their white caps for black ones.   I still
believe, however, that the gulls we saw were
the so-called " black-headed gulls " in their
winter plumage.   My critics were, I think, in
error as to the date of the occurrence, thinking
it took place on the 10th of April, the date
when the letter was written, whereas I witnessed the scene on the 22nd of March.
Now it is quite possible that, owing to the
severe return of winter, which took place in
March, 1889, mentioned in the preceding

letter (XXI.), in consequence of which the
river had risen in flood on the 22nd, that the
spring change in the birds' plumage had been
delayed.   I am very familiar with the little
black-headed gull, as my brother Robert
had one for many years ; and I knew that the
change in plumage was a very sudden affair.
In a letter to Mr. Ruskin, March 3rd, 1884,
my brother says : " My small black-headed
gull ' Jack ' is still flourishing, and the time
is *coming* when I look for that *singularly
sudden* change in the plumage of his head
which took place last March." (Italics mine.)
The birds I saw were so exactly like in shape
and size to my brother's bird that I am still
convinced that they were of that species.
My critics are both ready enough with the
Latin name of the bird (with which I did not
care to bother you), but neither suggests what
other sort of small gulls these that we saw
could have been if they were not the black-
headed ones.   After all, the fact of the matter
is, that when I wrote the correct name of the

gulls I saw was of very little importance
either to you or me, my purpose being, as an
artist, to convey to you, a brother artist, the
charming effect produced by the white gulls
and black rooks in the bright sunshine
feeding together in the shallow flood water
on the meadow. At the same time it was a
careless blunder of mine about the change of
plumage, and so no doubt I deserved correction.

Our Professor Anderson lent me some
extremely interesting papers on gardening
and flower arrangement amongst the Japanese,
which I have been reading lately; he also
kindly sent me a number of photographs of
gardens in Japan. It appears that the
Japanese approach flower culture and flower
arrangement with a sort of religious, artistic,
and scientific spirit, which is entirely unknown
to European nations. The following quotation
from a paper written by T. Conder, Esq.,
F.R.I.B.A., published by the Asiatic Society
of Japan, gives one an idea of the views with

which flower treatment is regarded by this curious nation.

"The high esteem in which the art has been held is illustrated by the following ten virtues or merits attributed to those engaged in its pursuit, namely :—

Koishikko.—The privilege of associating with superiors.

Sejijō jōkō.—Ease and dignity before men of rank.

Muitannen.—A serene disposition and forgetfulness of cares.

Dokuraku ni Katarazu.—Amusement in solitude.

Sōmoku meichi. — Familiarity with the nature of plants and trees.

Shujin aikiō.—The respect of mankind.

Chobo furiu. — Constant gentleness of character.

Sēikon gōjō. —Healthiness of mind and body.

Shimbutsu haizo.—A religious spirit.

Showaku ribetsu. — Self-abnegation and restraint." [1]

The following on the question of cutting flowers is interesting; you may remember that in one of my former letters, I said that in some cases it seemed to me a kindness to flowers to gather them, namely when the weather was vile out of doors. I was therefore pleased to read—

"The same Buddhist doctrine which forbade the wanton sacrifice of animal life is said to have suggested the gathering of flowers liable to rapid destruction in a tropical climate, and prolonging their life by careful preservation."

The whole of Mr. Conder's paper is of great interest, and he gives a number of pages of diagrams and line plans of Japanese flower arrangement; from which the extreme importance that the Japanese attach to line is very evident. Beauty of line appears to have

[1] Trans. of the Asiatic Soc. of Japan. Vol. XVII., Part II.

been made a most abstruse study of by these
curious people for generations.

All the lines with them have names and
significations, and certain leading lines are

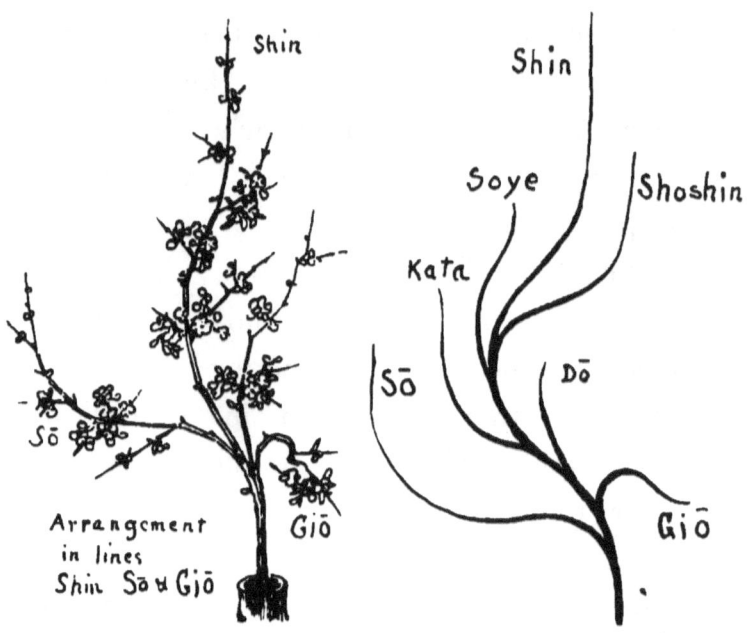

never absent from the arrangement. Here
is one, as an example, of a seven line arrangement.

The long centre line, Shin, is always

present as the predominant line in the composition, and the shortest, called Gio, is likewise never absent, though the character of
the curves varies a good deal according to
the number of the sprays employed. They
use small branches and sprays of blossoming
trees much more than we do, and select and
trim them according to the lines they are
intended to take in the composition.   In
every case line is everything, our bunchy
haphazard bouquet method being quite unknown to them or discarded as wanting in
taste.

They generally support these sprays by
fixing them into little heaps of stones at the
bottom of pans or vases of water. The
significance which these lines are sometimes
made to take you may judge of by this
example, called *De Fune*, it is the line
arrangement of a spray fixed in a hanging
piece of bamboo and is meant to represent an
outward bound ship. Similarly they arrange
lines in such a piece of bamboo to figure

a ship at anchor, in full sail, in a gale, home-
ward bound, &c., &c.

De Fune
(Outward bound Ship)

Judging from the photographs, the Japanese
garden must be pretty and very quaint.
They use much rock-work and stones of
large size. They are fond of pools of water
or small watercourses, with large slabs
of stone for bridges, the paths have often
little stone steps in them up and down ; they
clip and manipulate their bushes and trees,
but not in the solid formal manner of our old

gardens; indeed they seem to have a great feeling for wild natural arrangement which would delight Mr. Robinson's heart.

When any tragic event occurs in a small country town it is felt by everybody in a manner that is unknown to town dwellers. Yesterday there was a sad case of suicide here, and to-day the horror of the thing seems to be reflected in every face you meet; small crowds of townsfolk are all day long to be seen on the bridge staring at the boat-house in which the poor drowned body has been placed.

Much as I enjoy living by our river, the number of deaths by drowning that occur every year in our immediate vicinity is rather appalling. A policeman, who is fixed at Benson, told me that he had to attend six or seven inquests on an average every year at that place alone, all cases of accidental or suicidal drowning.

LETTER III

1st March, 1894.

MY DEAR MARCO—I think I never told you of the great loss we sustained in the death of our dear old favourite Rosie, which took place last October. She was only ill, apparently, for a day or two, and I was not anxious about her, as she took her coffee and some breakfast I gave her the day before that on which she died, and seemed decidedly better then; but on Sunday morning we found her lying on her side in the stable in a state of collapse. I sent for the vet., who came, but could do nothing except to pronounce that she was dying, in his opinion, as much from old age as anything else. I am inclined to think, however, that the extraordinary drought in the spring and summer (1893) had somehow injured her health, as she must have greatly missed the fresh grass, which was her chief diet. Her little paddock was completely baked up for three months, and she had to be fed on odds and ends from the kitchen garden. Her death was deeply lamented by all who knew her; she had many friends in the town besides ourselves, children and others frequently stopping to talk to her, and feed her through the railings of her paddock as they passed by. With the help of my boys I dug her grave, and superintended her funeral. I had, with aching heart, to break the sad news to Madame Maës, who sent me three white rosebushes to plant over the grave. I shall have to get a new donkey before next summer to work the mowing machine, but it will be impossible to get one so sweet and com-

panionable as poor Rosie. To thoroughly
enjoy and appreciate the full truth and
beauty of the relation between Sancho and
his Dapple, you should keep a donkey yourself and make a pet of it.

I was reminded of my loss by a letter I
have just received from an anonymous correspondent, a reader of my letters, enclosing
Buffon's description of the Ass. I suppose
Buffon would not now be looked upon as
much of an authority, but for graphic power
and truth the enclosed would be very hard to
beat. My obliging correspondent says of it :
" If it is not already known to you, you will,
I feel sure, enjoy it immensely ; if you do
know it, like all good things it will be none
the less good for being tasted again."

L'Âne.

" L'âne est un âne, et n'est point un cheval
dégénéré, un cheval à queue nue : il n'est
ni étranger, ni intrus, ni bâtard ; il a comme

tous les autres animaux, sa familie, son espèce,
et son rang ; son sang est pur, et quoique sa
noblesse soit moins illustre, elle est tous
aussi bonne, tous aussi ancienne que celle du
cheval. Pourquoi donc tans de mépris
pour cet animal, si bon, si patient, si sobre,
si utile ? Les hommes mépresent-ils jusques
dans les animaux, ceux qui les servent trop
bien et à trop peu de frais ? On donne au
cheval de l'éducation, on le soigne, on
l'instruit, on l'exerce, tandis que l'âne, aban-
donné à la grossièreté du dernier des valets
ou à la malice des enfans, bien loin
d'acquérir, ne peut que perdre son éducation ;
et s'il n'avoit pas un grand fonds de bonnes
qualités, il les perdroit en effet par la manière
dont on le traite : il est le jouet, le plastron,
le bardeau des rustres, qui le conduisent le
bâton à la main, qui le frappent, le sur-
chargent, l'excèdent sans précaution, sans
ménagement. On ne fais pas attention que
l'âne serois par lui-même, et pour nous le
premier, le plus beau, le mieux fais, le plus

distingué des animaux, si dans le monde il n'y avoit point de cheval : il est le second au lieu d'être le premier, et par cela seul il semble n'être plus rien.   C'est la comparaison qui le dégrade.   On le regarde, on le juge, non pas en lui-même, mais relativement au cheval : on oublie qu'il est âne, qu'il a toutes les qualités de sa nature, tous les dons attachés à son espèce ; et on ne pense qu'à la figure et aux qualités du cheval, qui lui manquent, et qu'il ne dois point avoir.

"Il est de son naturel, aussi humble, aussi patient, aussi tranquille, que le cheval est fier, ardent, impetueux ; il souffre avec constance, et peut-être avec courage, les châtimens et les coups ; il est sobre, et sur la quantité et sur la qualité de la nourriture ; il est fort délicat sur l'eau : il ne veut boire que de la plus claire, et aux ruisseaux qui lui sont connus : il bois aussi sobrement qu'il mange, et n'enfonce point du tous son nez dans l'eau.   Comme on ne prend pas la peine de l'étriller, il se roule souvent sur le gazon,

sur les chardons, sur la fougère, et semble par.
là reprocher à son maître le peu de soin qu'on
prend de lui : car il ne se vautre pas comme
le cheval, dans la fange et dans l'eau, il crains
même de se mouiller les pieds, et se détourne
pour éviter la boue : aussi a-t-il la jambe
plus sèche et plus nette que le cheval.   Il est
susceptible d'éducation, et l'on en a vu d'assez
bien dressés pour faire curiosité de spectacle."

I met Henry Moore on Tuesday at the
R.A., who told me the following pretty little
story in the bird line.   He was sketching one
day on the edge of an old quarry, on one side
of him ¸there was a steep sloping mass of
débris and tangled bushes, on this slope he
caught sight of what_looked like a gray ball,
moving in an eccentric way.   He clambered
down and caught the fluffy mass in his hands ;
it proved to be two tom-tits in deadly con-
flict ; so eager were they in their animosity
that they never attempted to separate, and
were caught quite easily.   Moore thought he
would take them home to examine them at

his leisure, so he carefully folded them up in a red silk handkerchief and put them in a loose pocket of his great coat. When he got home, however, he was much surprised to find that they had both escaped, the handkerchief was still carefully folded but a large hole had been pecked through it. Considering that it was a silk handkerchief this work of the tits seems to me very remarkable and clever.

We have had a delightful winter this year, the majority of days being mild and bright, and the frosts of brief duration. The rains have not been of a persistent character, though there have been many violent gales of almost phenomenal force.

LETTER IV

12th March, 1894.

DEAR MARCO—Hearing that some rather
curious mural decoration had been found in
two old cottages which were being repaired and
altered at Crowmarsh, I went over there on
Wednesday to see them. The building had
been originally one house, not by any means
large, built in the Tudor period, and probably
always used as a farmhouse. Some time ago it
had been divided into two cottages and dis-
connected altogether from the farm-buildings
which belonged to it.

I made some rough memorandums of parts

Mural Decoration, from a Cottage at Crowmarsh.

of the decoration, which I enclose. The room
in which this decoration was found is quite a
small room, on the upper floor, next the roof;
the decoration consists of a sort of bordering,
running all round the walls next to the ceiling,
its width is about one foot, and it is apparently on the broad beams, which form
what are termed the plates, on which the
rafters rest.   These beams are a little over a
foot in width and had been painted in tempera
of a cream colour; on this the patterns are
worked in brownish colour.   The execution is
very vigorous and evidently entirely free-
handed; it is varied throughout, with no trace
of stencil anywhere.   The interest of this work
is in the evidence it bears to the generally
prevailing artistic taste in the 16th century,
when we find such a small farm-house in the
country thus decorated.   I do not believe the
whole work took very long to execute; it is so
free and bold that I should say that it had been
begun and finished in a day; probably most
house-painters in those times could easily

have done work of a similar character. The artistic character and freedom of this decoration contrasted painfully with the cheap little

Ben

wall-papers with which the lower rooms of the cottages had just been adorned.

I know you are not such an ardent dog-lover as I am, I trust therefore you will pardon me for boring you about our little dog "Ben." He is a mere puppy still, sixteen

months old, but with great character and
clever qualities.   He takes me out for walks
in the afternoon (as all good dogs should
their masters), and his great delight, when we
reach the open arable land which surrounds
this town, is to start off at full speed, in the
mad endeavour to catch a lark.   He runs
with his nose to earth, like a fox-hound, and
as the birds spring up right in front of him,
I have no doubt he hunts by scent.   He
takes no notice of other birds, such as rooks,
starlings, or sparrows, which most puppies
chase.   I am inclined to think that larks are
rather game birds, and leave a strong scent.
He lays his nose to earth and starts off
running when no birds are visible, but as he
runs the larks keep rising before him, right
in front of his nose.   I have read somewhere,
I think, that larks are more numerous in
Great Britain than any other birds, and I am
disposed to believe it.   Of course there is
an enormous quantity of sparrows, but the
sparrow confines himself chiefly to the

immediate vicinity of man, whereas the lark's
habitat is spread over the broad land in every
direction.   In the winter I have sometimes
witnessed the partial migration of larks; a
broad continuous stream of birds from N.E. to
S.W. which flew overhead uninterruptedly for
nearly twenty minutes.   I was told these birds
go to the marshy lands about the estuaries
of our southern rivers.

Yesterday we were out with the dog about
sunset, there was a cold west wind blowing,
the sun going down in a clear sky, just after
a slight shower with its accompanying rain-
bow.   When we reached the open fields Ben
started off at once hunting, though at the
time not a bird was to be seen anywhere ; but
it was astonishing to see him put up larks
in every direction as he "scoured awa' in
lang excursion," at times quite out of sight.
Many of these, when thus disturbed, began to
rise and sing, but not in the upward circling
manner which they do in the midday sunshine.   As far as I could judge there seemed

a pair of larks on every twenty yards square
where the dog ran.

During this walk, whilst the before-men-
tioned shower was going on, we sheltered by
a wall with overhanging ivy on it, just opposite a rookery ; the wind was blowing fiercely

A Rookery in a Gale.

and the nests on the tops of the elms
swayed about in a way which suggested sea-
sickness, or that the eggs might roll out or
get addled. Beside each nest its two pro-
prietors were perched, all of them head to

wind, reminding me of a fleet of luggers at
anchor. They seemed to hold on with great
ease. The sight reminded me of a fact about
birds, which Sir Edwin Landseer once pointed
out to me, namely, that all birds, when perched
on trees or bushes, serve as weather cocks, as
they invariably arrange themselves head to
wind. He told me that he found this fact
most useful in deer-stalking, as he could always
determine which way the wind was blowing
on a distant hill, a most important knowledge
in deer-stalking, by observing the birds with
his field-glass. The reason of the bird's
position is easily understood when we consider the set of its plumage and call to mind
the ridiculous and uncomfortable objects our
domestic poultry look when running, as sailors
say, before the wind, their tails blown open
over their backs and the birds almost blown
off their legs.

March came in this year as a lion, but
thank goodness a west wind lion, and the
proverbial peck of dust is at present wanting

owing to the succession of showers which
alternate with bright sunshine. It is not
exactly April weather, as the rain generally
lasts for five or six hours with equal intervals
of sunshine. I am getting in a good stock of
oxygen in preparation for the selection work
at the R. A. next month : here, at any rate,
I escape the importunities of the " Artists'
Parasites " with which my town-dwelling
brethren are so grievously afflicted at this
season.

LETTER V

16th March, 1894.

DEAR MARCO—I get a large amount of pleasure from my little greenhouse, especially in the spring, when, though the sun shines often enough, the keen winds prevent me from enjoying the outdoor garden. I have no heating apparatus to this house; on the whole I think it suits me better without. I know what an enlarged scope artificial heat gives to one's horticultural and floricultural operations, in the way of grapes, orchids, ferns and hot-house things in general; but I get as many grapes as I want given me by kind neighbours, am not an admirer of the eccentric character of most orchids, and prefer hardy plants that give no trouble to any exotics that require cosseting.

All these luxuries entail besides the dirty and disagreeable work of stoking, either on yourself or on a gardener ; if you do it yourself, unless the glasshouse is the only sort of garden you possess, the time taken up by it will be too great ; if you leave it to your gardener (that is, should you keep only one and a boy as I do) you will be sure to find that he will very soon spend the greater part of his time pottering about the house, neglecting the outdoor work, or leaving it to the boy as much as possible. Whenever you happen to visit the glasshouse it is almost a certainty that you will find him already there, or that he will come in directly afterwards. The place will be no sweet sanctum of your own, so that at last you will get into the custom of visiting the place only on Sundays,

when the gardener ceases from troubling.
I believe that most gentlemen who keep a
large staff of gardeners and have much glass
seldom see the inside of their hothouses
except on Sundays, and probably have very
little knowledge of, or control over, what
is grown in them. My little greenhouse is
"a poor thing, but mine own," and in it I can
carry on any sort of fooleries I like in floricultural, or other, experiments without dread
of interference.

On a bright sunshiny bleak day in March
the temperature inside the place is delightful,
the mere sun heat being of a pleasanter
character than when hot pipes are employed.
These always seem to me to give a damp,
stuffy atmosphere. By the way, it was only
quite lately that I learnt how it is the sun
heat accumulates under glass; I had a
vague idea, as I dare say most ordinary
gardeners have, that the glass somehow
drew the heat, and that was all; I had in
fact never considered the fact seriously. My

son, however, who had studied physics, gave me the proper explanation ; it is simple enough, just as the explanation of a good conjuring trick always is ; it is owing to the fact that glass allows *luminous heat* to pass through it readily, but is a bad conductor of *non-luminous heat ;* so the heat gets caught inside the house in a sort of trap, the light carrying the heat through the glass and there leaving it to shift for itself to get out again ; thus it becomes stored, being continually accumulated as long as the sun shines.

I do not attempt very much in my glass-house ; the back wall is devoted to my fig-tree, and in lieu of the usual stand for pots in the front I have a solid bed of rich soil three feet deep, in which I can plant anything I like. There is a large tank for rain water in one corner, and some shelves to carry pots close up to the glass.

My fig-tree is a great success, it now nearly fills the back wall, and I have to prune it every year, cutting out the old wood

and training the young in its place.   Just
now the buds are bursting at the ends of the
shoots, the young leaves unfolding themselves
in the cleanest and neatest way imaginable ;
they are most fascinating things to watch day
by day.   The young figs are already of a
lovely colour and considerable size.   This
tree gives me little trouble and quantities of
fruit ; a little manure in the winter and plenty
of water in the spring is all I have to give it.
It yields abundance of fruit, the first crop
beginning to ripen in June, and going on
until the second crop comes on, so that I am
able to gather a few figs nearly every day from
the end of June to the middle of November.
There is always enough for all of us, and as
we are all very partial to the fruit, that means
a good many figs.   I get a few dishes of
early strawberries from some plants in pots,
they bloom about the end of March, and as
few bees come in then, I fertilise the blossoms myself with a paint brush.   I used to
grow tomatoes in the front bed, but I gave

them up, as they required a good deal of
looking after, and kept the sun from the fig-
tree ; besides which I found that they did far
better in the open air.   I now have in this
front bed one or two clumps of chrysanthemums, they are of good ordinary sorts, dark
red, yellow, and white ; they have not been
moved for four or five years, and nothing
done to them except cutting them down in
the winter, adding a little top dressing each
year, and watering freely in the summer ;
otherwise they are left entirely alone to grow
at their own sweet will, and very well they do
it, rising to the glass roof, bending over,
down, and up again in beautiful and graceful
curves, intertwining with one another in
inextricable confusion, and at length blooming in numberless clusters, which, when
gathered entire with long stalks are extremely
decorative for the house.

I have no bother in striking, potting, re-
potting, tying up, disbudding, placing out of
doors, carrying them in again, fumigating, or

messing with liquid manure. No doubt the sight of my wild-looking plants would drive a professional " Mum "-grower frantic ; but I maintain that the large free *clusters* of bloom ·that I pick in November, are far more lovely in their grace and variety, than any of the huge solitary fatted up things which one sees at shows, and which are little better than gigantic rosettes, each on a thick stem by itself, tied stiff and stark all the way up to a stick. Four or five such at times occupy one pot, but in every case all the natural graceful tendency of the plant is severely repressed and thwarted by a whole year's laborious meddling with nature. It is the old old story, monstrosity usurping the place of beauty, the wonderful and the monstrous appealing to the great majority of minds so much more forcibly than the beautiful.

I make further use of my glasshouse by starting annuals in it in pots and boxes, also providing my wife with pans of mustard and cress from time to time. Here, too, I study the ways of my toads and sundry other creatures, and here I hang up and keep my own particular trowels, shears, and other gardening implements which would otherwise get appropriated by the man or the boy.

When I receive any parcel of new plants it is here that I unpack them, here too I pack presents of flowers or plants for my friends. Altogether the place has become to me almost as enjoyable a structure as my studio itself, the feeling that I ought not to be wasting my time in it adding greatly to the intensity of my enjoyment.

On a drive to Ewelme last Wednesday I saw quite a flock of Yellow-hammers by the hedge on the roadside, their bright plumage looking very pretty as contrasted with the gray hedge. They kept up with the carriage for quite a long distance, flitting up and across and back over the hedge just in front of us.

These birds are peculiarly fond of this

sort of game.   Why do they do it ?   When
it is only a pair of birds that perform these
antics one naturally supposes that it is done
to divert the attention of the passer-by from
the situation of their nest ; but here was a
flock of a dozen or more apparently engaged
in mere play ; they seem to enjoy letting you
approach quite near and then popping away
over the hedge to appear again a little farther
on.   I have often seen swarms of gnats keep
up with me along a road, and the river-flies
will sometimes travel long distances in company with a boat, but for what purpose I am
quite at a loss to imagine.

LETTER VI.

16th April, 1894.

DEAR MARCO—I returned from the selection of pictures at the R.A. on the 11th, having been sitting with the others for eight days judging some 15,000 works. Alas! alas! As bad luck would have it, I thus missed the first burst into bloom of an *Iris Susiana*, to which I had been looking forward with great eagerness. This iris is very difficult to manage in our fickle climate. It is six years since it bloomed with me, then it did so in the open garden, but I have never

succeeded in repeating this triumph in the
open air, and this is the first success after
many failures, even under glass. This iris
in its native land is generally covered with
snow during the short sharp winter, and
makes its extremely rapid growth during the
short spring which follows; after blooming
it endures the long baking drought of summer, which ripens the tuberous roots thoroughly. Of course, in our country such an
arrangement in the open ground can hardly
be expected, and though when planted in the
open the tubers thrive and grow amazingly,
they make in our damp autumns far too early
a start, throwing up a number of strong green
blades which are almost always doomed to
destruction by the lasts frosts of winter, without showing the least sign of bloom. The
books say that they require some protection,
such as a handlight, in the winter; but I have
tried this over and over. again without the
slightest success.

In my little greenhouse, however, I think I

have mastered the difficulties of its culture at
last. My method is to defer planting until
very late in the autumn ; I put the tubers
into rather a small pot of nearly pure river
sand, this pot I place inside another larger
one, and plug the space between the pots
with dry moss. I place the pots on a shelf
in the sunniest part of the greenhouse, and
give no water at all until some time after
Christmas. Strange to say the green shoots
often begin to show before the plants have
received a drop of water. I give the water
very liberally at first, but in great moderation
as the plant shoots into growth. I let it have
all the sun that shines, and if the frosts are
very severe at any time I take the pots into
my studio whilst the extreme cold lasts. This
year my treatment has been quite successful,
and the plant burst into bloom on the 4th
of April, whilst I was still from home. My
wife told me that when she entered the greenhouse in the morning the sight of the two
blooms quite made her start, and well it might,

for I can safely say I know no flower that
approaches this in individuality, sombre
majesty of colour, or dignity of form.

It is called commonly " the mourning iris,"
on account of its sombre grayish colour, a
gray to which it is quite impossible to give a
name ; the standards, as the upper leaves of
an iris are called, are large, round, and beautifully laced with this dark gray ; Gerard
says, " like unto a guinea fowl's plumage,"
but this is scarcely an accurate description.
These standards form a sort of arching canopy
over what I should call the working parts of
the flower, possibly protecting them from extreme heat.   The falls, or lower leaves, are
darker, the markings being closer, with an
almost black velvety spot in the centre, which
is surmounted by dark fur.   The wing-like
covers to the entrance to the ovaries are also
of the darkest shade.   The blooms are very
large and much more globose in shape than
the common German iris.   I hope you will
forgive me for boring you thus about this

G·D·L

IRIS SUSIANA.

[To face page 44.

flower, and kindly make allowance for the
enthusiasm of a gardener, who has been
struggling for six years with Nature, when at
length his efforts are crowned with success.

All the irises are lovely, but this one far
surpasses all others that I know, in the mysterious glamour that it inspires when seen by
any one for the first time. The little *Iris
tuberosa*, or snake's-head iris, approaches
I. Susiana, in my opinion, perhaps nearer
than any other in fascinating interest. This
iris has been beautifully described by E. V. B.
in her delightful book *Days and Hours in a
Garden ;* it is, like the mourning iris, sombre
in tint, a mixture of olive, brown, velvety
black, gold and green, that is exceedingly
harmonious, the foliage is long and narrow,
the small blooms are at first wrapt up so tightly
that they hardly show, and the flower itself
is so small that to see its quaint beauty one
has either to stoop down or pick the bloom.

This iris is hardy enough ; if the spring is
fairly mild, and the curious little bulbs are

planted in a sheltered place near a wall, it
never fails to bloom.   But you will have to go
and look for it, as its humble size and sombre
colour render it invisible to all but those who
have eyes to see, and know how to use them.

It promises to be a good season for my
tulips, they are mostly of the late blooming
varieties, Parrots, Gesner, and the old-
fashioned long-stalked sorts that flourish
usually in cottage gardens; the only early
tulip I have is the Turkestan tulip or
Tulipa Greigi, which came into bloom here
on the third of this month; this magnificent
flower might well be termed king of all tulips.
I know of none that approach it in size and
brilliancy; when it is fully out its colour is of
the most dazzling orange vermilion, but it is
even more beautiful in colour before it is fully
expanded.   I measured two huge buds, and
found they were each a trifle over five inches
in length, which is enormous for a tulip of
any sort.

This tulip is very hardy indeed; its foliage

is curiously variegated with chocolate-coloured spots ; it is one of the first bulbs to shoot out above the ground, and snow, frost, and rain harm it not. It is just the tulip for my garden, where things get left alone, and rest in peace from year to year, as it does better for being undisturbed ; these bulbs of mine have been seven years in their present place, and are this year finer than ever I remember them.

On Sunday the 8th I found my two toads swimming in the tank in the greenhouse, it was the first time this year that I had seen them, I cannot say how long they might have been in the water, but it was impossible for them to get out again, the water being low in the tank, and the tank having an overhanging flange on its top edge, so I placed a board sloping down into the water, which they availed themselves of, for the next morning they were both beneath the root branches of the fig-tree. I did not look for them again until the 14th, when I could only find one.

This one appeared profusely covered with moist exudation, and on examining it closer, I discovered that it was in the act of changing its skin ; the animal raised itself on its legs at intervals and strained itself in some way so as to render its body very thin and gaunt ; in these efforts its eyes, which generally protrude considerably, closed and sank down to the level of the rest of its head.

The old skin seemed very flexible and glutinous, but a small portion only remained when I saw it, just about the head and shoulders ; it was dragging this forward with its forepaws and cramming it into its mouth. I watched until the whole was swallowed. After the operation the markings on the new coat were very strong and bright, and the beast seemed exhausted, utterly refusing to take the least notice of the wood-lice that I placed for it. The next day its coat was dry, and, with the exception that the markings were still rather conspicuous, it had regained its usual appearance. The mention of wood-lice reminds me that I received a letter some time ago from your brother John in which he tells me, apropos of a note in one of my former letters, as to woodlice being called "God Almighty's pigs," that his wife told him that her brother, Fred Walker, and her sisters when children, always called these animals "old sows," and that they had the name from an old gardener.

I have not much in the way of bird news for you. On the 13th at lunch-time we had the treat of seeing a little cock-tail wren perch on a honeysuckle close to the dining-room window, flit his wings, cock his tail, and sing several times with unmistakable signs of joy and exultation. I mention this as a treat, as indeed it was, but it is also an event to note, because it is so very seldom that these dainty little birds ever allow you to catch more than a momentary glimpse of them as they flit and creep amongst the hedges and along the old walls ; the

E

song is something like that of a robin but much shriller and more hurried.

The cuckoo has already (April 16th) been heard here, but not by me. I have heard, however, the wryneck, which is called "the cuckoo's mate." Hook told me that the country people regard the first note of this bird as a warning that the proper time for peeling the oak-bark has arrived, they think that the bird says " Peel, peel, peel, peel, peel."

LETTER VII

30th April, 1894.

DEAR MARCO—People may be held fortu-
nate who strike up friendships with plants
and flowers early in life, for unlike other
friends, these never grow old or desert us,
but return each year with their sweet faces
unaltered.   One of my earliest acquaintances
amongst flowers is "the Jew's Mallow," or
Kerria Japonica, and yet I had lived for
more than fifty years in familiarity with it
before learning to name it correctly.   It is, I
suppose, an introduction from Japan, but it
must have been introduced into England a

E 2

long time ago, for it is a very old and estab-
lished favourite in cottage gardens almost

Kerria Japoncia.

everywhere; I cannot, however, find any
allusion to it in Gerard; its name " Jew's
Mallow " is ambiguous and misleading, for it

is in no sense a mallow. It acquired this
name by a mistake, for formerly botanists
had named it *Corchorus Japonica* from
its similarity in appearance to *Corchorus
olitorius*, a Syrian plant, used by the
Jews as a pot-herb, and hence the name
" Jew's Mallow." *Corchorus capsularis*,
another species, very similar in appearance,
is the plant from the fibre of which jute is
made. Our plant, however, is of a different
natural order, that of the roses, belonging
to the genus Kerria. It is generally seen
as a climbing wall shrub beside a cottage
door or summer-house. I only know it in
its common or double yellow form, though
there is a pretty single one, and I believe
a white variety. Its flowers look very like
small tufts of orange wool, the leaves are
pointed, much serrated, and of a warm
green colour, their surface is rendered dull
by deep corrugations. Though I was never
properly introduced to this Kerria until a
year ago, I have known and loved it ever

since I was six years old. The front garden
of the house in Pine Apple Place, Edgware
Road, where I was born, was separated
from the next-door garden by a light iron
railing; this plant was in our neighbour's
garden against this railing, so that we had
the benefit of its beauty on our side as well;
yet though we continually broke the tenth
commandment as to the flowers, I do not
remember that we ever broke the eighth;
this was not so much owing to our moral
principles as to the awe with which we
regarded our neighbours. They were unknown to us except by name, all of them
"grown up," solemn and sedate, not to say
grim, in character; the plants grew in direct
view of their parlour window, and it would
have been a risky thing to have put our
little arms through the railings after the
flowers. The first death, I ever recollect,
was that of the head of this family next
door. The funeral was an awful thing as
viewed by us through the slats of the

venetian blinds. The undertaker's men
took large plumes of feathers out of black
bags and stuck them in the horses' heads
and on the hearse. Two "mutes" stood
on guard at the door with what looked
like brooms wrapped up in crape. Horrible and gruesome was the garniture of a
funeral in those days, as no doubt you will
remember.

I overheard my nurse saying that the poor
gentleman had died from a sore throat
("bronchitis" was not invented then), from
which I gathered that a sore throat was
a mortal complaint and certain death ; and not
long afterwards, when my own throat may
have been a little relaxed, I recollect I lay
awake nearly a whole night, in fearful misery,
expecting death at any moment.

The sight of this little yellow flower still
always recalls to me our old front garden and
our mysterious neighbours ; and it is rather a
curious fact that during all the years that have
intervened, I have never got any nearer to

the plant than my neighbour's garden, for it
never grew in either my father's, my mother's
or my own gardens, whilst in all the gardens
next to all these it has invariably flourished.

There is at present a fine plant on the
summer-house in my neighbour's garden, and
D.V. I will really have one in my own before
next year. Another equally old friend is the
Japan Quince, sometimes called *Camelia
Japonica*. This has grown, I am happy to
say, in all my gardens, and lives and thrives
with me still. My human living friends, of
fifty years standing, I can now, alas! count
easily on the fingers of one hand; how
changed in appearance are even these! whereas the "old familiar faces" of the flowers
once loved remain the same year after year,
young and beautiful. These old friends are
to me the *real flowers* with which I am con-
tent to live and die; I never feel much
longing for the brilliant novelties, which are
yearly announced and figured, in gaudy
colours, in the nurserymen's catalogues. I

THE EDGWARE ROAD, SEEN FROM No. 12 PINE-APPLE PLACE, IN 1835.

From a picture by C. R. LESLIE, R.A.

[*To face page* 57.

wonder whether the son of an enthusiastic
orchid-grower would feel in his old age
as much love and delight on meeting with
orchids that he had known in his father's
glasshouses as a child, as I do with my well-
remembered garden friends. I suppose he
might possibly ; but though I went into plenty
of conservatories and hothouses as a child, I
never entertain the same feeling for exotics
as I do for this Kerria, Japan Quince, and
all the other dear old hardy friends of my
youth.

When we lived in Pine-Apple Place, there
were hayfields in front of our house ; so
pretty was the view from our parlour window
that Constable presented my father with a
round mirror, to hang opposite to the window
so as to reflect the green fields and hedge-
row elms. Hamilton Terrace was all grass
then, and Abercorn Place a mere country
lane, from the sides of which the wild Con-
volvuluses, that my father introduced into his
picture of *Perdita* were gathered. Cherries

and peaches ripened well in our garden, to say
nothing of apples and pears.

My eldest sister was a first-rate gardener.
She kept bees too, and knew her flowers
thoroughly and well ; of these we always had
plenty. We younger ones had also little
gardens of our own, and thus it was that I
imbibed an early and true love for flowers, by
which I mean not only delight in them as
beautiful objects, but also the pleasure to be
found, and found only, in tending to their
culture personally, and watching the phases
of their growth and nature from year to year.
All the flowers that grew in that old garden
I have now in my new one along with many
others, but none are so dear to me as the old
favourites.

This is, I am afraid, a sentimental letter,
but I trust you will pardon it, for it is a wet
day and I am all alone, which may in some
way account for it.

LETTER VIII

22nd May, 1894.

MY DEAR MARCO—It has often been re-marked that farmers are a grumbling lot and never satisfied under any circumstances, but I think, from my experience of them since living in the country, that they certainly do not deserve this character. I have, on the contrary, been much struck by the manly patience with which they have lately struggled on through these years of agricultural depression ; and really, when one lives in the country, as I do, with a small garden to look after, you soon find cause to sympathise with the farmers in their complaints as to the fickle character of our climate.

I am not fond of grumbling at the weather, as no doubt it is better ordered than if we had the management of it, but one cannot get over with equanimity the disasters that occur every now and then through the sudden changes of climate to which our islands are peculiarly liable. Last Thursday everything in my garden was in the most promising condition ; we had had plenty of nice rain, the temperature had gone up ; the irises and pœonies were in full bloom, roses were in bud, indeed my Maréchal Niel was in more than bud ; the columbines were well out and a host of other perennials making a fine show. The lilacs were nearly over, but the hawthorns and laburnums shone out in glory against the blue sky ; birds sang in every tree, the young starlings in their nest in the sycamore tree were screeching and squealing all day long, and I walked in the evening to Shillingford to hear the nightingales. But alas ! on Fri-

day the wind began to whip round to the
N.E., the sky, it is true, remained clear, but
little by little the wind grew stronger and
colder, whilst clouds began to appear and rob
us of much sun heat, and on Sunday night
there was a hard frost which was repeated on
Monday night, and the catastrophe was complete.

Now all my irises are shrivelled up, and
the oriental poppies have blackened petals
and drooping buds.   Some lovely tender
sprays of *Heuchera sanguinea* which had just
begun to bloom, and which were the very
pride of my heart, are all bent double and
burnt up past all hope.   Two beautiful sprigs
of blossom on a buck-bean in my bog garden
are reduced to a loathsome brown mass.
These, for a few samples of the havoc
wrought amongst my flowers, will suffice ; in
the kitchen garden, all my potato halms have
turned from a healthy green colour to that of
withered seaweed ; the young kidney beans
are in much the same plight, their broad

leaves hanging over and lobbing about like a row of drunken men. Young marrow plants are reduced to absolute nothingness, and so on, and so on, everywhere you look.

The cruel wind seems to fall away to a calm towards evening and the nights are clear and bright; towards morning there is a thick white mist and at six o'clock the grass and roofs are white with frost. The sky is cloudless at first, but about eight o'clock the old persistent devil-wind begins again bringing with it paltry gray clouds and the day is passed in alternate intervals of scorching sun and cold rain or sleet. You in town would only notice the cold, but here, we are painfully alive to the widespread misery and loss such weather brings.

No doubt but that the birds must suffer too; Peter brought me yesterday two dead swallows, which he picked up by the boathouse, no doubt killed by the cold. I can only hope that they were a husband and wife, so that only one family may have suffered.

There is a County Agricultural Show about to be held in the meadow opposite our house, on the other side of the river; the whole field has been enclosed with hoarding and filled with tents and sheds, &c., which to-day look gay with flags.   It is to be opened to-morrow. There are some small elm trees enclosed within this hoarding, in which usually sundry woodpigeons build; the birds I expect have been scared away by the preparations for the show, which have been going on ever since the beginning of April, and have come over to my garden, where they, I believe, have built some nests.   I do not know exactly where their nests are situated, but one or two of these large birds are always about the walnut tree and in the shrubbery near my studio. They remind me of the members of the Senior United Service Club when they are driven over by the annual cleaning to take refuge in the peaceful halls of the Athenæum.   I recognise these birds as fierce and distinguished strangers immediately,

when they start out of my shrubbery with
tremendous slapping of their powerful wings.
They are wonderfully heavy birds and seem
to fly with considerable exertion.   It is quite
possible that their nests may be low down and
easy to find, for I saw last year, in a friend's
garden, a woodpigeon sitting close on her
nest in a thorn bush, not more than eight
feet from the ground ; the bush itself grew at
one corner of a tennis-court on which games
were played continually, and the bird would
allow people to look at her without stirring.

I received an interesting letter from a very
old friend who resides at Lewes, in which
were notes on one or two subjects mentioned
in my former letters ; he gives a receipt for
making proper food for young birds, such as
I described in Letter XIX.   It is, "ground
oatmeal rubbed through a fine sieve, so as
to get rid of every particle of husk, which
would otherwise choke them ; mix with this
a small portion of almost any kind of sweet
biscuit, and add a fresh snail chopped very

fine. Make this about the consistency of
pap, feed every two or three hours, of all
things early in the morning. With almost
all descriptions of small birds (other than
thrushes) the oatmeal and biscuit alone ; food
fresh every day." He says, "With regard
to robins, I have observed that they frequently, after nesting, leave the old quarters
and are not seen for three or four months,
but are sure to return as winter approaches,
that is to say, the one—seldom two old birds
—never more." He also adds as to what I
said of mushrooms (Letter XIII.) : " I assure
you the farmer's account to you of the pro-
duction of mushrooms was no matter of
superstition, but, I have no doubt, a matter of
fact. But an even surer way of getting
mushroom-spawn, would be to have an entire
horse in your stable for a week or a fortnight,
and put down in his bed some old rotten
sacking, and leave it to be saturated ; the
more rotten the better, then make up your
mushroom bed, and I venture to say that you

F

will get a fine crop of mushrooms." I should
not care to have such a horse in my stable
for a fortnight, but I may try the experiment
some day, as a friend of mine near here has
one or two fine stallions; if I succeed I will
let you know.

LETTER IX

7th June, 1894.

DEAR MARCO — Yesterday I drove to Swincombe to look at a collection of old family pictures belonging to some friends of mine. The day was rather like one in March than June, but I enjoyed the drive notwithstanding, as the country out in that direction is very beautiful. The Chilterns are the high range of chalk downs that are situated in the south-eastern corner of the county of Oxford; they differ from most of the other chalk downs in the south of England, in that they are plentifully wooded and

F 2

studded all over with villages, farmsteads,
and gentlemen's houses and parks. The
western and north-western flanks of these
hills are by far the most beautiful in variety
of scenery. On this side, along the entire
range, huge downs jut out like promontories
into the plains below. The extremities of
these spurs are generally two or three miles
apart, but at their bases the little valleys
between them contract into most picturesque
secluded combes. In these, if any one wished
to live in seclusion "far from the madding
crowd," could be found most charming re-
treats of natural loveliness. In one of these
combes, "Swincombe," the old house is
situated, where were the pictures I went to
see. The tops of these jutting spurs are
more or less devoid of wood, though most
of them are dotted about with juniper bushes,
and some have on their summits isolated
clumps of trees which are in this part of the
country called "Cuckoo Pens." I suppose
pen means a hill or peak, but how cuckoo

comes in I know not ; they speak of " Swincombe Cuckoo Pen," " Brightwell Cuckoo
Pen," and so on.   Swincombe Down itself is,
I think, one of the grandest of any of these
promontories, the view from the top being
very extensive.   High Clere Beacon can be
easily seen from there, over the tops of the
Compton Downs.

In the woods on the side of this chalk
down numbers of beautiful wild flowers are
to be found, of those kinds of course which
love a calcareous soil, many of the rarer
kinds being met with.   Here I picked one
or two blooms, though I am sorry to say not
quite full out, of helleborine (*Epipactis
Grandiflora*) just about the time that the race
for the Derby was being run and won on
another celebrated chalk down in Surrey.   I
thought the helleborine would have opened
in water and a warm room, but it did not,
and I drew it as it was ; it belongs to the
orchis tribe, and is very graceful.

The agricultural show on the meadow

opposite our house is over, and the hoarding
which surrounded it, and which spoilt the view

Helleborine.

from our windows ever since the beginning
of April, is at length down, and made up into

parcels of wood which are to be sold by
auction on the spot.

The show was of the usual character of
that sort of thing; what pleased me most
were the little black Kerry cows, which were
not much larger than . Du Maurier's St.
Bernard dog, they should have had red halters
instead of white, to have set them off properly.
The riding and jumping competitions were
very exciting, one cannot help feeling proud
of a country that produces the plucky young
centaurs who take these jumps, over a stiff
hedge with a broad piece of water beyond it,
and who remount again and again after failures
until they succeed. There was a lady
amongst them who jumped everything in the
boldest way. There were a great number of
shire stallions exhibited, to say nothing of
bulls and rams, and as these animals were on
the field for a considerable time, I shall be
curious to see if any mushrooms appear this
autumn.

The weather this year seems to be making

up for the dry season last year with a vengeance. I should not mind it so much were it not accompanied by such persistently strong winds, mostly from the north. The hedges and trees everywhere show the effects of the two nights of cruel frost on the 20th and 21st of last month. Our walnut tree was a special sufferer, and indeed everything came badly off in my garden, except, perhaps, the monthly roses on the trellis, on either side of the path to the boathouse. These seem to have escaped bravely, the cold in some way adding to their colour and prolonging the duration of the bloom. The rain is, however, very troublesome, loading the boughs of bloom so heavily, that they hang about in a most untidy way; I relieve them every day, as well as I can, by gently shaking off much of the wet, but still they scarcely recover their proper places. I am afraid to allude to this trouble to my gardener, or he would at once go down the rows and ruthlessly bind the straggling shoots back to the trellis with tarred string, in

hideous bundles.   There are two things which
I believe no hired gardener ever can or will
do properly, namely, tying up and weeding.
When he does the latter he " worrits " about in
the most disastrous manner with fork, hoe,
and rake, hoofing all your bulbs and seedlings,
bent only on producing great expanses of tidy
but bare mould.   Nothing can persuade him
to use his fingers or to stoop.   And, as to
tying up, his only idea is to plant a stake
right down into the very heart of the plant's
roots, and bind the wandering sprays up into
a bundle like an old Gampy umbrella.   I have
only one man and a boy, but even that is bad
enough, and I envy not those wealthy people
who keep scores of gardeners, for they can
scarcely call their gardens their own.   In such
gardens these minions seem ever present,
bobbing up from behind the different bushes
like " Clan Alpine warriors true " on every
side where you least expect them ; every walk
and border is haunted by its real master,
every greenhouse has its man in possession.

Sundays and the late hours of evening are the only times on which the real owner can enjoy his possessions in peace.

I have to do this tying up and weeding mostly myself, and my hands are hardly ever without scores and scratches from the thorns. Still it is better so, and after all it is astonishing how little needs really to be done. Roses of all things resent interference, and it is wonderful how well they do when left alone. Of course if large show specimens are wanted pruning is essential, but these are gained by the loss of all glory of growth. I have a hardy climbing rose that has grown up into a tall fir tree, covering it with its bloom, which has a charming effect as seen from the upper windows of the house. An unpruned rose-bush may look, to some, untidy, but the number of blooms more than compensates for everything.

LETTER X

15*th June*, 1894.

DEAR MARCO—I was gathering some roses the other day, to send to a friend in town, my little girl Lydia was helping me, I regretted to her how few white ones there were in the garden, but I remembered that I had just received a present of two nice roots of a rose called " La Reine Blanche," whereupon Lydia wanted to know why they so often give roses French names. It is not a very easy question to answer. All the roses with French names were not originated in France,

numbers of them have been bred in England.
I rather think it is because we English have
not sufficient poetry or imagination to give
pretty names to our nice things ; so we write
our dinner *menu* in French, and any new
fashionable colour is generally introduced
under a French name.   In old times we were
a little more proud of our nationality and
displayed a certain amount of good taste in
these matters, some of our old-fashioned roses
still retaining their very pretty names.   " the
maiden's blush," "eglantine," "five sisters,"
"the velvet" and "moss rose."   But it is
rather sad that nowadays when English names
are provided not. only for new roses, but for
many other flowers, generally denominated
"florists'," that our national snobbishness
should so much prevail.   Thus we have Dukes
of Albany, Edinburgh, Connaught, Teck, and
Wellington, Baronesses and Countesses of this
and that, and Mr. Gladstones, &c., without end,
with hosts of names of people of lesser or no
fame at all.   One rose is called " Lord Bacon,"

which is wrong and foolish, because there
never was such a person, the supposed author
of Shakespeare being " Francis Bacon, Lord
Verulam." Now and then we come on a
name of the good old sort, as, for example, ·
" Pride of Waltham," " Queen of Queens,"
or " Fair Rosamund."

When these snobbish names are given to
what are called " Florists' Flowers " I do not
regret it so much as in the case of the roses,
as I am not a great admirer of most of the
florist's pets. Begonias, gloxinias, show
chrysanthemums, and some others give me
no delight ; the natural flower amongst such
plants has generally been tortured out of
existence by persistent and tasteless interference. Even our roses have been, I think,
a little spoilt by cultivators. The dog-rose,
sweet briar, or the damask being still far
ahead, in pure loveliness, of the whole herd of
modern bred roses. One forgives a cabbage
or a moss rose for not showing its golden
stamens on account of its delicious perfume,

but many of the huge hybrids at our shows
cannot plead this excuse. I hope the time is
not far distant when prizes will be given for
the best exhibits of open roses of all sorts ;
and that by the judicious crossing of such old
favourites as the damask, the Macartney,
the Persian, and the Austrian briar, &c., we
may arrive at some pretty varieties to which,
let us hope, good old English names may be
given.

No roses in a garden pay better, for the
little trouble that they give, than the common
China rose. A very dear friend of mine, for
whose taste in flowers and gardens I have
the greatest veneration, advised me, when I
first took up this place, above all things to
have plenty of these delightful roses. I
have ever since felt grateful to her for having
given me that advice, and thankful that I
followed it.

On either side of the brick-paved path that
leads from the drawing-room door to the boathouse, I planted rows of China roses, sup-

ported by low trellis-work. None of the
arrangements that I have effected in my
garden have been more successful, or met with
greater admiration, than these rows of China
roses. They have been planted for about
twelve years, and though I have never done
anything to them except occasionally cutting
out dead wood, and tying up here and there,
they are finer this year than I ever remember
to have seen them. They are hardly ever
touched by blight of any sort, they yield
many more clusters of bloom than any rose I
know ; they go on blooming, as long as the
weather is at all mild, even up to Christmas-
time ; nothing is prettier than a bunch of
their half-open buds, with their foliage, picked
late in the autumn ; cold weather seems to
add a deeper hue to their colour ; this year the
cold wet weather and the frosts did them
rather good than harm, as their colour never
was finer, and the first blossoming time has
been prolonged.

The weight of the raindrops on their boughs

gave me some work, as I mentioned in my last letter, but it did not injure the flowers otherwise; whereas numbers of the fatter blooms of my other roses, Maréchal Neil, Gloires, and General Jacquimenots were rotted in the bud by wet. I give only a slight top dressing now and then to the narrow borders in which these roses are planted, which has to serve for them and sundry other plants, chiefly aquilegias or columbines, which grow, mostly self-sown, from year to year, closely over the rose roots. I have read in some rose-grower's book that roses resent having plants above their roots, but I believe from repeated trials and observation that they resent much more having only bare earth; anyhow my roses and columbines get along in perfect accord. These columbines are chiefly crosses between *A. cerulea* and *A. chrysantha*, infinitely varied in their colour and form. Great numbers of bulbs lurk beneath the columbines such as crocuses, scillas, tulips, and daffodils, which put in a cheerful appearance in the spring; none of these are ever touched, but still the whole bed goes on from year to year, and as far as I can see without deterioration anywhere.

In an adjoining garden, kept by a retired engine driver, is a border still more crowded than mine, roses, lilies, columbines, pansies, Canterbury bells, and many other perennials, are in the bed, and against the wall an apricot tree, a peach, and a Maréchal Neil rose. This bed is never dug or touched with hoe or fork, and is densely packed, but still the roses bloom in perfection as do the white lilies and all the other plants, whilst the crops of peaches and apricots are simply splendid.

It is but fair to state, however, that the wall at the back of the bed is that of a malt house, which has a furnace at work in it during the winter; that the aspect is due south, and that the soapsuds, from the Mondays' wash tubs, generally go on to it when the weather is dry.

On one side of my trellis of roses, where

G

the lawn slopes away, I have a thick hedge of
lavender, it grows bulging out, and covers a
sloping bit of grass which used to be rather
difficult to mow.

This arrangement of mine meets with more
approbation from visitors than anything else
in my garden, whilst the roses, the trellis and
the lavender afford me constant satisfaction
from the sense of permanence they give the
place.

LETTER XI

2nd July, 1894.

DEAR MARCO—My garden is, I think,
to-day in the very zenith of its beauty ; but
as much of its extra glory is due to the
poppies, which are very fine this year, I
am afraid that it will not last very much
longer in its perfection.   I never try to keep
up appearances after July, chiefly because, as
the boys' holidays then commence, it is quite
impossible to prevent the devastation occasioned by the hunting for tennis balls,
romping. and games of all sorts, that take

G 2

place. So my garden gets a holiday in the
autumn, as well as the boys. It looks a little
untidy, I admit, but it is a better thing for
the perennials to let them die and shed their
seed naturally, than to tidy them up, and
cut them down, in order to make room for
autumn flowers. I am no very great admirer
of the usual autumn flowers, such as zinnias,
dahlias, China asters, &c., they are very
bright and gay, it is true, but lack *delicacy*
of beauty. My untidy beds, however, are
not entirely devoid of bloom, as there are
plenty of Japanese anemones, tall phloxes,
asters, colchicums, &c., with monthly roses,
and sundry hardy things which keep on
blooming away until the frosts come. In
October and November I go all over my
borders, cutting down, dividing, altering,
&c. ; giving here and there a top dressing
of leaf-mould and manure. Bonfires at that
time of the year hardly ever go out, the
scent of which has ever been delightful
to me.

My garden has been wildly luxuriant this year, a perfect jungle, but a jungle of flowers, owing to the frequent showers and moderate sunshine. Tying up was out of the question as there was no place anywhere to step amidst the thick growth; so the plants rambled as they liked and supported one another, indeed they had no room to fall down; the result being an intermingling of blooms, as varied as it was beautiful. Columbines and campanulas grew up into the rose bushes; nasturtiums, cornflowers, poppies, and snapdragons, all of them self-sown plants, filled up every vacant place. Whilst character and individuality was kept up in different places by plants of large habit, such as sea hollies, globe thistles, tall mulleins, and white foxgloves, alstrœmerias, acanthuses, bocconias, centaurea macrocephala and others; the last-mentioned is a very picturesque subject, having very large thistle-like flowers, which look rather like bunches of yellow silk growing out of fir cones. Weeds have this year had little chance, as they found no bare places left for them to grow in, and what few sow thistles or nipple worts there were I easily got rid of by that most useful of all garden tools, a long-handled spud of this shape.

There were, however, some dismal failures this year, notably amongst the lilies, which suffered severely by the cruel frosts on the 21st and 22nd of May. The strawberries too were utterly ruined, we have none, neither will there be any walnuts or mulberries on my trees.

You know well how few people there are who, when they come into your studio, know the proper place in which to stand from which to view your pictures. I recollect, in old times, on " Show Sundays " you and I used to place obstacles in the way to prevent

people from standing in the wrong places,
and how even then they would repeatedly
move these obstacles.   It is really astonishing how ignorant the generality of people
are about the simple principles of seeing
things rightly.   I have to take just the
same care when I am showing friends the
flowers in my garden, as I do when they
come to see my pictures in my studio, I
generally conduct them cunningly to the
best points of view before directing their
attention to a flower border.   In a garden
it makes all the difference whether the
spectator has the light behind or in front
of him.   When the light comes through the
border towards you every petal and leaf is
enriched by transparency and the colour
intensified, whilst if the light is behind you
and shines dead on the objects in your front
the effect is cold and opaque.   You might
as well look at a stained glass window from
the outside in order to judge of the beauty
of its colour, as at a bed of flowers with the

light coming from behind you.   When walking through fields with the sun on one side
of you the grass on the side that the sun
is on looks far richer in colour than it does
on the other side ; in fact the whole landscape is richer and stronger in effect when
the light comes *through* it to the spectator,
though the other aspect has great beauties
of its own as well.   The early morning is
by far the best time of the day in which
to see a garden in perfection, the rays of
the sun are then low and horizontal, and,
therefore, as they come across the flowers
towards you, the transparency of leaf and
petal is doubly intensified, added to which
the flowers themselves are fresh and lovely
after their night's rest and adorned with
glittering dewdrops.

A few days ago I made the acquaintance
of a little bird that was new to me, namely,
the redstart.   The afternoon had been very
wet and warm, at about six o'clock the rain
cleared off and the sun came out, everything

looked glittering and beautiful, when my attention was called to an extra amount of twit-twit-tit-tit-titting in the shrubbery. There were several tomtits about, but I also caught sight of two little birds amongst them, about

The Red Start.

the size of a flycatcher, very active, with gray backs, russet wings, black bibs under their bills, white crests on their foreheads, orange tawny breasts, and more or less orange tails. One might have imagined them to have been crosses between a robin and a tomtit. They flew about from tree to tree, flirting their tails as if to show off the orange feathers in them. One flew very close to me on to the pole of the tennis-net, and from thence on to the lawn to a place where I had smashed an ant heap. I watched them for some time with my glass from the boathouse window, and saw them feeding on a low wall that keeps up one of my borders, which has many ants' nests about it. I made a little sketch on the spot, whilst my recollection was fresh, which I send you. I then consulted dear old Bewick; found out that the birds were red-starts, and that they fed much on ants and their eggs. Bewick scarcely gives the active brisk look that the birds I saw possessed, in his representation. Peter tells me that he has often seen these birds in the garden, but it is strange that I have never noticed them before, and I do not believe that they nest here, or I think that I must have noticed them. I fancy possibly that they are attracted by the numbers of small field ants' nests that abound in my lawns and on the old walls that keep up the river frontage, and that these birds pay us occasional visits for feeding purposes. I am the more inclined to this view of the case as it appeared to me, when I first saw them, that the tomtits were resenting their intrusion as strangers, which accounted for the twit-tit-tit-titting that I heard.

LETTER XII

20th July, 1894.

DEAR MARCO—On a recent visit to my friend Mr. Fisher, of Winterbourne, near Newbury, I saw a very interesting example of what botanists term "an escape." The little brook "The Winterbourne" for about two miles of its length, is at present thickly planted along its edges with mimulus, or monkey flower, which has at some time or another found its way to the brookside by seed from a cottage garden near the head of the stream. When I first noticed the luxu-

riant blaze of yellow flowers, I took them
for marsh marigolds, but as it was in July of
course these could not have been in flower.
I never saw any naturalisation of a garden
flower more complete. The plant had taken
thorough possession of the fringes of the
brook, from the little village of Winterbourne,
all the way to where it joins the Lambourne,
near Donnington Castle. I did not see any
after that on the sides of the Lambourne, but
no doubt the steeper banks of this much
larger stream prevented the seeds from
finding a congenial root-hold. The smaller
brook flowed along down a rather steep
course without any definite banks ; it ran
through long grass, clumps of water-flags,
masses of water-cresses, forget-me-nots, and
other aquatic plants, amongst which this
mimulus seemed to be very much at home.

It is evidently a semi-aquatic. I never
cared for it much as a garden plant, it being
generally rather dwarf and dowdy-looking,
but when it found so congenial and natural

an environment as this brook-side afforded, it
presented a very much more vigorous and
effective appearance, and I at once saw how
nature had intended the plant to look, and
where it should grow and flourish. It was a
very good object lesson on the importance of
giving any plant in your garden, that you
wish to see in perfection, as near an ap-
proximation as you can in soil and situation
to that which it would have in its wild natural
state.

In a good-sized spinney near Mr. Fisher's
house the " Lily of the Valley," *Convallaria
majalis*, grows in the utmost abundance.
This is a native of our country, though rather
scarce, and as the little wood in which these
that I saw grow is well away from any garden,
I have no doubt but that they have flourished
here undisturbed from time immemorial.*
Mr. Fisher, whose father had the house and
farm before him, knows nothing as to their

* Gerard says the " Convall Lily " grew in his time on Hampstead Heath, "fower miles from London," in great abundance at
Lee in Essex, and on Bushey Heath and many other places.

ever having been introduced here. The whole wood is thick with these lilies, and in the spring Mr. Fisher's daughters gather any quantities.

I am not, as you know, a great admirer of the vast panoramic views that are obtained from our hills and high downs, but that which is seen from High Clere Beacon, near New-bury, is certainly one of the most beautiful I ever saw. Lord Carnarvon's park, with its magnificently wooded undulating grounds and lakes gives the foreground on one side quite a romantic appearance; the tower of the house looking very like a cathedral one.

The whole Kennet valley with its water meadows and the downs behind it is on the north, the Surrey hills to the Hind Head on the east, and right away to Winchester on the south; the intervening spaces being covered by innumerable farmsteads, pasture land, and gentlemen's seats. The whole forms a pano-ramic view of lovely pastoral scenery, peace-ful in character, and rich in historic interest

and association, such as can only be found in
our own dear country. Such views as these
always cause me to feel rather sad, possibly
because one cannot help the foreboding that,
all this simple character, these hedge-rows,
thatched cottages, barns, and all the rest of
the picturesque and lovable features of old-
fashioned agriculture, must before long give
way, that the inevitably slate roof and tall
chimney will take their place, and that, beyond market gardening beneath glass, and
some dairy farming, agriculture will cease to
exist for us in England.

A lady reader of my former letters sends
me some interesting notes about bees ; perhaps you may remember when you and I
were at Ramsbury Manor house, the bees
had taken possession of the roof of an
old out-of-the-way garden summer house,
and that an old man told us that these bees
had forsaken their regular hives for this place,
because the bee master had neglected to
inform them on the occasion of a death in

the family belonging to the manor.   He said
that it was a well-known fact that bees if
they were not told, by knocking on their hive
and by the voice, of a death in the family,
would either die or leave their hive.   I can
scarcely believe this to be more than a superstition, founded on an occasional coincidence,
but here is a plain statement of fact that at any
rate is curious.   My lady informant writes :
" There is a remarkable superstition (?) that
obtains in Hants, and I think in all bee-
keeping provinces, viz. that on the decease of
any member of the family, a man has to go
round to the bee-hives, tap them gently, and
tell them of the death, or else the bees will
die before the next swarming time.   That they
die if *not told* I have proved to be a fact in
my own family, and the only explanation I
offer is, that by or through the wonderful
instinct of the bee, it divines that there is a
shadow of misery over the home they are
connected with, which so overclouds their
sensitive nature, that they need the reassuring

mesmeric touch of the human hand and voice to keep them in health or life. On the death of my youngest son, —— came to ask me if he might go tell the bees ; not understanding the old custom of that county I marvelled, but said 'yes,' it was done and the bees remained ; but on the death of my brother, some time afterwards, though I counselled the same, the matter was 'pooh-poohed' and the bees all died."

This lady also gives evidence as to the fact that bees will not sting those people who are fond of them and who are not afraid ; that such people can handle a swarm, without any protection on their face and hands, without getting stung, I believe to be quite true, as my second son, when at Marlborough, used regularly to help his master to hive his bees, when they swarmed, with no protection on, and he told me that the bees hardly ever stung him, and that even if they did, accidentally, the sting gave little or no pain. My lady informant further writes :—

" Hants is especially a county for bees, the immense clover fields yielding them glorious feeding grounds. The Rev. E. Hawkins, late rector of Overton, Hants, used to have a bee-carriage into which he lifted his hives, and drove with them many miles to pasture them ; camping out with them several days. The bees would return at nightfall to their own hives in the bee-carriage on the strange camping ground which was eighteen or twenty miles distant from Overton."

No doubt you remember the swarm of bees that had taken up their abode in the old dis-used chimney in Fred Walker's garden in St. Petersburg Place. Walker used to put a little pan of water for the bees to drink from and would never allow the bees to be disturbed ; there must have been a great many as they had been there many years without ever throwing off any swarms, and were an immense time in returning to their hive in the evening. I remember a swarm of bees that hived themselves in the ceiling of a billiard-room in a house at East Sheen. They no doubt had been there for many years and at last the weight of the honey broke down the ceiling, and the whole mass falling on to the table quite spoilt the cloth.

LETTER XIII

22nd August, 1894.

DEAR MARCO—On the 9th of this month,
when I was inspecting the walls of our old
church of St. Leohards, in my capacity as
churchwarden, my attention was drawn to
the vast number of small snails which were
adhering to the surface of the walls, chiefly
on the south or sunny side, though there
were a few on the north side as well. I am
much puzzled as to the object these little snails
can have in thus climbing the walls and apparently remaining there torpid for so long ;

I have looked at them several times since and
find that they are still all there.   They are
nearly all of one sort ; of a pale cream colour
with black stripes on their whorls.   At first
I thought that they were dead or that the
shells were empty, as when I picked them off
the animal was scarcely to be seen ; but I
afterwards found that it had only drawn itself
up into the innermost coils of its shell.   All

that I squashed had the snail inside them, but
still I thought that they might be dead or
dying until a day or two ago when I took
some home to draw for you ; I put these on
my drawing board, flat, and drew one ; but
the next day, when I came to look at the
board, they had all righted themselves and
had crawled to some distance.   I cannot
imagine what could be the purpose of these

snails thus spreading themselves out on the walls—it could not be for food, for the walls were entirely bare of vegetation ; neither could it be in order to collect lime from the walls, as there were quite as many on the glass windows and the iron piping. The grass in the churchyard was long and moist, amongst it were plants of the common wild mallow on which I found several of the same sort of snails feeding. It was far too early in the year for them to have been in search of hybernating quarters ; it was also rather too late in the year for them to have crawled there for breeding purposes. Snails do not mind rain in the least, or I should have thought, as we had been having a very wet season, that they had climbed the walls to dry and sun themselves ; possibly they had been increasing the growth of their shells and climbed the walls to rest themselves and to harden their shells in the sun and air.*

* I looked at these walls on the 28th September, 1895, and found that there were still a number of snails on the walls then, though perhaps not quite so many as on the 8th of August the year before.

I have frequently noticed that the common tabby snail at times, during the summer months, takes to mounting walls and odd places, resting apparently on the elevated situation for a considerable time; they generally seem to choose angles, where two walls meet, or some shelter or ledge, and almost always select a dry bare wall. The dryness of the wall leads to their destruction, in my garden, for the dry wall shows up their track and directs my attention to them.

I have often seen long tortuous tracks of snails over bare walls and even on the inner walls of sheds and outbuildings.

In the breeding season I have seen these snail tracks in a very marked manner; once I followed such a track and found a snail at its end that had met another coming from an opposite direction, the two sharing a sudden and ignominious death.

It is astonishing what a distance snails will travel. I have known them travel more than half-way across my tennis court, in the

middle of the day, in the hot sun, a very
exhausting process, as they continually leave
a track of slime behind them.   In the night-
time, when they usually travel, no doubt
they could go very much farther as the
ground is damp with dew and easier for
their mode of progress.

Moorhens are very rightly named, as they
are not only very like our domestic hens
in aspect and way of walking and feeding,
but their cry also greatly resembles that
of our hens.   The commonest noise that
they make is a sharp jerky one which sounds
like chĕckgrĕc, but they have also an alarm
or danger cry which is not at all unlike that
which a hen makes when it is being chased
or caught.   Young moorhens cheep just
like little chickens, and when older, and
they get driven away by their parents, I
have heard them make just the cry or plaintive cheep that large chickens do about the
time that they are cracking their voices.

This year the old saying about St. Swithin

has come curiously true, to-day is the only
entirely dry day that we have had since the
15th ult.   Next Friday is St. Bartholomew's
day.   There is an old saying about that day as
well, which though in horrible metre runs thus :

> " All the tears St. Swithin can cry,
>   St. Bartlemy's dusty mantle wipes dry."

St. Bartlemy's day, however, is the 40th
after St. Swithin's, so perhaps it is only
the natural end of the spell.

We were visited last week by a strolling
company of actors, who had an ingenious
method of advertisement.   The company were
here three days ; the proprietress walked
about the town, shopping and distributing
hand-bills, followed by a large dog with a
coat on, on which was an advertisement of
the play ; a young donkey with a collar
round his neck also followed his mistress,
with the dog, entering all the shops and
houses that she did, no doubt getting fed
and petted every now and then.   It was a
very droll and rather pretty sight.

LETTER XIV

24th October, 1894.

DEAR MARCO—As I have had to be in
town four days a week during this month,
doing duty as visitor in the schools
at the R. A. I have had little leisure
to make notes on anything that would
interest you. I saw a tern on September
26th, hawking up and down over the river ;
it was quite alone and only stayed one day
near here. There seemed to me to have
been a greater number of wagtails on our
lawns during September than usual ; these

birds have a sharp jerky little note which sounds like "chipsit." At times they will rise in the air, making a momentary hover, after a fly, very much in the style of a flycatcher; sparrows will sometimes execute a similar manœuvre but in a far clumsier fashion. The gray wag-tail is almost as common about here as the pied one; it has a pretty yellow throat and breast; they seem particularly fond of the edges of the river.

When you think what a clumsy thing a bat is in appearance, is it not marvellous how extremely rapid its flight is? Their wings and general structure are so totally different to those of the swallow, and yet they catch and feed on very much the same prey. Though they have not the swift dart of the swallow they fly very quickly, doubling and turning even more rapidly and suddenly than the birds do. As they have no tail their steering must be effected entirely by their wings, which are divided into sections by

their long slender finger-bones, and I suppose
that the partial closing, or extra expansion,
of one of these sections would cause the
animal to turn very suddenly. This is my
theory, but as they fly so irregularly and
rapidly it is quite impossible to ascertain
accurately how they manage. I once picked
up a little bat which had a slit in the delicate
web of a section of one of its wings, it
could hardly fly at all in consequence of this
damage; I put it in as secure a place as I
could find, thinking that perhaps with rest
the rent might be repaired, but I am
afraid that the creature perished after all.

On a wet day I often sit·in the little room
over the boathouse, and watch the effect of
the rain on the surface of the river. Provided that the wind is moderate in force, just
enough to ruffle the water, the rain and wind
together give the surface the look of dull gray
frosted silver. But I dare say you may have
noticed that there are, in different places,
certain perfectly smooth shiny parts inter-

mingled with the general roughened surface.
These are always long strip-shaped pieces,
flowing out with the stream, which keep continually altering their curving forms.   I cannot account for these smooth places except by
supposing that they are due to some kind of
oil on the water ; my reason for this supposi-
tion is that I have noticed they very frequently have as their starting point some little
patch of rushes or weeds ; these rushes, I
believe, as they get stirred by the wind set
free an oil from the mud around their roots,
which rises to the surface and flows off down
the stream.   The fact that tiny streaks of
smooth water can be seen below even solitary
rushes lends strength to my theory.   That
the rushes cause the smooth places by the
shelter they afford from the wind cannot be
entertained, as these streaks of smooth water
flow always from the rushes down stream
even when the wind is blowing directly up.
These markings on the river surface, during
rain, have, as far as I remember, never been

indicated by landscape painters, though they
are very beautiful in nature, forming fine
graceful lines on the dull gray surface and
likewise helping to give the level look by their
perspective ; but when I come to think of it
landscape painters very seldom paint the effect
of rain on a river at all.

Though we have had such a cold, wet
summer, it is curious that my acanthuses
bloomed magnificently.   These plants, with
me, are very shy bloomers ; I have had them
now for over six years in my garden, and this
is only the second time that they have
bloomed.   They are very handsome, throwing
up huge spikes of bloom, the character of
which is just what I greatly admire, having
plenty of quaint construction.   They retain
their form, like the teazle, far into the autumn,
when the seed pods swell up beneath a sort
of little roof of a purplish colour ; this first
forms part of the beauty of the flower, and
remains unchanged until the seed is nearly
ripe.   The whole plant bristles with sharp

spines, which suggest a connection with the
thistle tribe, but the plant is no relation to the
thistles ; the spines are differently disposed,
being confined to the points of the bloom
spikes, and to the tips of the numerous
divisions of the leaves and not on the stalks
or stems. These spines are very sharp, their
prick being irritating to the skin. The foliage
is remarkably beautiful, it is the plant which
is supposed to have suggested the ornamental
leaves on the Corinthian capital. Though
not very hardy in our climate, the roots hardly
ever die, but I believe it never blooms in the
summer that succeeds a very hard winter. It
is common in Greece and the Holy Land ; my
nephew brought me some dry blooms from the
latter place, where, he told me, he at one time
rode knee deep through masses of the plant.

I am quite at a loss to account for the
curious name sometimes given to the acanthus, viz., " Bear's Breech." Gerard does not
much help me on this point ; this is what he
says :

"The tame or garden Branke Ursine is
named in Latin Sativus, or Hortensis Acanthus, in Greek παίδερος : and of Galen,
Oribasius and Plinie μελάμφυλλας : Plinie
also calleth this Acanthus lenis, or smooth
Branke Ursine, and reporteth it to be a citie
herbe and to serve for arbors : some name it
Branca Ursina (others use to call Cowparsnep
by the name of Branca Ursina). The Italians
call it Acantho, and Branca Orsina : the
Spaniards Terna Gignante : the ingravers of
old time were wont to carve the leaves of
this Branke Ursine in pillers, and other
workes, and also upon the eares of pots, as
among others Virgill testifieth in the third
Eclog of his Bucolickes.

> Et nobis idem Alcimedon duo poculo fecit,
> Et mollis circum est ansas amplexus Acantho."

At this season of the year, when the steam
launches and holiday people have ceased from
troubling, the river is very delightful, and I
enjoy taking my little dog with me in the
punt of an afternoon ; I land him on the bank

I

and he seems never tired of hunting for water-rats. Kingfishers are much more frequently seen at this season, and their beauty is intensified by the subdued tones of the willows and rushes. They have a sort of shrill whistling note which is very pleasing, especially when two are together and hold conversation. I am afraid that I shall have very little more boating this year as the wind is blowing strongly from the south, with driving rain which will cause the river to rise.

LETTER XV

20th November, 1894.

DEAR MARCO—No doubt you must have
thought of us when in your morning paper
you read accounts of the great flood that has
been going on in the Thames Valley for the
last fortnight. It has been the highest but
one of any flood during this century, the
water having risen to within nine inches of a
recording mark on a stone at Shillingford,
put up in 1809, which was the date of the
great flood that carried away the centre
arches of Wallingford Bridge. I have often

I 2

looked at this recording stone, in hot summer weather, with extreme incredulity, but there is no doubt, I feel sure now, as to its truthfulness.

The water did not, I am happy to say, come into our house anywhere, except in the cellar, beneath the kitchen, where a barrel of beer was lifted off its stand and carried away to some remote corner from whence it has not yet been recovered.

The width of the gravel path was all that was between the rising waters and the doors of our house, on the evening of the 15th, when the flood was at its highest; but there was a rise of another foot and a half above the path before the level of our floors could be reached, so I felt tolerably comfortable in my mind, such a further rise being almost impossible to imagine. My studio, in the cottage next door, was in greater danger, as the floor there was only six inches above the water level, and I was hard at work all Thursday morning putting such things away as might get injured upon chairs and tables ; the next day I could not get to my studio at all without wading knee-deep, as the boat could not enter the narrow passage that led to the door. The flood here reached its extreme height on Thursday the 15th at 10.30 p.m., at which hour it distinctly ceased to rise. No perceptible fall took place, however, until Saturday the 17th.

A flood is not a noisy and terrific demonstration of the forces of nature, like a thunderstorm or a hurricane, but it has an appalling character of its own, in the quiet, stealthy, irresistible way with which the waters rise.

I could not help wondering of how much use were now the new ugly iron flood-gates that have taken the place of the picturesque wooden weirs ; and of what had happened to the new sewage works at the various riparian towns ; ours were flooded, the man holes burst open, and the sewage escaped into the river as of yore ; at Maidenhead, I believe, the whole sewage outlet was entirely submerged.

When one viewed these mighty volumes of
water it seemed a little ridiculous that, only
quite recently, the sufficiency of the Thames
supply of water for London had been a
subject of debate. If only a part of the
superfluous water, which comes to us nearly
every autumn, could be stored in a large lake
above Oxford, in the water-meadow district
between Eynsham and Lechlade, it seems to
me that the water question for the metropolis
would be settled. It would be far wiser, I
believe, to *make* a new lake than to *spoil* a
beautiful old one in Wales; neither would
it be so expensive, as the labour employed would be chiefly that of the spade,
which is the cheapest of all, it can be
done by any sort of men, even by the
unemployed.

As far as I have been concerned with the
flood I have rather enjoyed it than otherwise, the weather, ever since the 15th,
having been warm and lovely, with bright
sun and moonshine, the sunrises and sun-

sets across the vast expanse of waters being extremely beautiful ; each night the moon shone brightly, so that I could go out over my garden in the little rowing punt and enjoy the extreme beauty and novelty of the effect.

The boathouse was, of course, a mere island, the water covering the floor of the little tea-room to the depth of six inches ; all the things in it had to be raised on tables and ledges. The tennis-court was covered by four feet of water, and formed a lovely calm pool to boat on. I took the opportunity in my boat of clipping the top of a hedge which was rather too high to reach under ordinary circumstances.

The moorhens made themselves quite at home amongst my shrubberies and kitchen garden. I noticed that all the birds seemed rather cowed by the unusual circumstances ; though they stuck to the place they appeared to miss the ground with their accustomed runs ; this was most noticeable in the case of the little

" Jenny Wrens," which are generally very shy of showing themselves ; they were now quite as tame as the robins, letting me have many opportunities of a good comfortable look at them.

On Friday I was in my punt with my little dog, over a corner of the tennis-court, when *our* kingfisher (for I feel sure it was the one that haunts this place continually) came and perched on a branch of the birch tree, not more than three yards from my boat ; it did not appear in the least afraid, but stayed there quite three or four minutes, putting up its crest, pruning its wings, and enjoying the bright sunshine ; whilst I could admire its exquisite plumage at my leisure. It then flew up the avenue of the shrubbery, and from thence on to a small apple tree in the kitchen garden, where I followed it in my boat, getting again quite close to it ; it seemed scarcely to notice either me or the dog at all.

My two eldest boys came down from

town on Saturday and we rowed out *across*
the river for quite half a mile from our
house, which looked at that distance more as
if it was on the banks of Southampton Water
than on the Thames. It is neither difficult
nor dangerous to navigate a small boat in a
flood to any one who is a tolerable waterman,
and who knows the ground well ; punting is,
however, out of the question, it being impossible to cross the deep stream with a pole.
The best boat to use is a small fishing punt
fitted with oars, as it draws little water, is
easily turned, and will go anywhere. I
rowed up to the bridge and even through it ;
the view from it was very fine, the river
being one vast lake right away to Streatley
Hill.

Yesterday, the 19th, the water had fallen
rather more than four feet, and I walked
over the tennis-court to inspect the state of
my flower-beds. I picked a large bunch of
monthly roses, which had been nearly but
not quite submerged during the high water ;

they were none the worse for it. The lawn
looked sodden and dirty ; the daisies on it
seemed to have been much perturbed by
their immersion ; all their little smooth green
leaves, which generally lie so flat and tight
on the ground, were raised straight up to the
sky ; it looked as though, feeling the water
over them, they had raised their arms up as
a drowning person does. I do not know
how to account for this action on the part of
the daisies ; no other plants on the lawn had
done the same, not even the plantains, but
every single daisy leaf was standing straight
up, looking very curious.

Very little damage was done by the flood
in this place. The bridge had to be reached
by boats from either end, as the roads to
it were under water. There were some
cottages near the river badly flooded ; one
man caught a large perch in his sitting-room.
I am happy to say that he was such a true
sportsman that he gave the fish its liberty.
But, with the exception of these cottages

and parts of some roads being flooded, and
the overflow of the sewage into the river,
Wallingford escaped wonderfully well as compared with Reading, Windsor, and Maidenhead, in which towns the damage was very
great.

LETTER XVI

30th November, 1894.

DEAR MARCO—The river has quite subsided again into its proper bed, the wind has
shifted to the north-east, and our poor farmers
have been getting on with their autumn
sowing, which was so long deferred by the
incessant rains.

Beyond a slight coating of sandy mud on
those parts which were submerged, my garden
looks just as it usually does at this season in
other years. The subsoil is very porous,
chiefly gravel and sand, so that the ground
dries up very quickly.

To-day is lovely and bright, and I made a careful inspection of my borders, marking out places for some new introductions, and putting in some bulbs that I had been prevented from planting earlier by the flood.   Here and there I found sundry tennis balls that had floated out from the hiding places in which they had lain since the summer ; it is needless to say that they had been nice new balls when first lost.   I looked into a little wooden hut, that my youngest boy had built beneath the walnut tree, and found that it had stood the flood bravely, though the wall-paper and internal decorations had suffered considerably. In this little hut in the summer holidays my children used to have small parties, when they would roast potatoes, fry kippers, and make tea on a small stove, enjoying themselves greatly.   An ugly bathing shed with a corrugated iron roof, which our corporation had put up on the river near here, did not fare so well as my boy's structure, for it was lifted bodily off its bearings, carried some

distance by the flood, and left lying across a
hedge a total wreck.

We shall miss an old familiar friend next
year from the banks of the river, between
here and Benson, namely an old willow stump,
of most quaint and picturesque appearance,
much like some fearful dragon or antediluvian
monster.   It stretched for many a year hori-
zontally out over the water, and must have
attracted the notice of every passer-by.   Last
summer, as two young ladies and their brother
were seated on it, it suddenly gave way, and
subsided gently into the water ; the young
ladies were not displaced when it fell, but
came down with it, seated, with their legs in
the water.   After this it remained there by the
river bank for some weeks, and, luckily, I
made a drawing of it as it looked in the water,
which I send you.   With the first rise of the
flood in November, the log floated off and
came down the stream, past our house, looking
more weird than ever.   It was landed by a
fisherman, who made it fast to a stake on the

OLD WILLOW STUMP.

[To face page 126.

bank and had just begun cutting it up for firewood when the water rose again and carried it off, where to I know not.

It is astonishing how plants will go on struggling into blossom in the late autumn as long as the weather is mild. I never worry my borders at this season by digging or tidying up, and as I make it a rule to have nothing in them but what is absolutely hardy, there are always at this time numbers of odds and ends of flowers from which to pick a nosegay if the frost keeps off. As there seems a likelihood of a sharp frost to-night I thought I would make a list of such blooms as I could find before that event takes place. You will understand, of course, that all the flowers in this list are not perhaps very fine specimens, though many of them are quite respectable ones.

Mignonette, snapdragons, marigolds, Campanula pumila and persicifolia, Aubrietia, Veronica reptans, Virginian spiderwort, Japanese anemone, stocks, nasturtium, scabious,

larkspur, *Tropeolum tuberosum, Ecremocarpus,*
globe thistle, acanthus (of these last two,
young second blooms), *Nigella damascena,*
scarlet Geum, *Linum flavum, Aster ericordia,*
sweet peas, the large St. John's wort, violets,
primroses, and pansies.

I have not mentioned the monthly roses,
the hardy jasmine *nudiflora,* or the laures-
tinas, all which are usually in bloom at this
season.

The other flowers I mentioned with the
exception of the violets were mostly in beds
above the line of the flood; the violets had
been deeply submerged, but they are now
blooming in numbers. As to the pansies
they seemed to take no more notice of the
flood than they do of the snow; I have some
good sorts, and also an enormous quantity of
little self-sown degenerate specimens which I
have never the heart to eradicate as weeds.
They are most persistent little plants and are
hardly ever out of bloom. It is these little
pansies that I selected for the design on the

cover of my book ; they seemed to me appropriate for that purpose, having to other and more elaborate and distinguished flowers just that same sort of relationship which these letters of mine have to works by authors of more authority.

Design from the cover of *Letters to Marco.*

Still these little pansies are not weeds, they claim the right to be considered as flowers, flowers too which are the emblems of thoughts, and, in this sense, the somewhat plaintive motto beneath them is appropriate.

K

LETTER XVII

28th December, 1894.

DEAR MARCO—Until now we have had nothing but mild weather, but this morning there was a smart ground frost, so that I fear it will not be long before the discomforts of winter will be upon us in earnest.

On Christmas Day a friend brought us a pretty bunch of primroses and one cowslip, which he had picked in the morning in a wood about four miles from here. I picked a number of charming buds from my monthly rose-bushes on the same day; on the 24th, I

G.D.L.

WINTER HELIOTROPE.

[*To face page* 131.

picked our first winter aconite, to-day there
are quite a number out in the shrubbery.
The winter aconite, with us, is far earlier than
the snowdrop, and I always regard it as the
first flower of the new year ; its claim might,
however, be disputed by another plant, the
sweet-scented colt's-foot, or "winter heliotrope" as it is sometimes called, which in
sheltered places puts forth pretty heart-shaped
leaves and a curious insignificant-looking
head * of bloom which has a strong and sweet
scent.

The aconites, however, are far more showy
and spring-like in character than this colt's-
foot, which is somewhat of a weed—in fact
a relation to the butter burr. Besides, the
colt's-foot gives in entirely at the first hard
frost, leaves and bloom shrivelling to a
blackened mass, from which it hardly ever
manages to get out another bloom during the
winter. The aconites, on the other hand, will
remain above the ground frozen for a week

---

* Botanists call it "a racemose panicle."

or more, and when the thaw comes go on
with their blooming as if nothing had happened. The snowdrop and the crocus do not
show so suddenly as the aconite, there is little
to be seen of them but a tiny streak of white
or yellow between their narrow leaves for
days after the flower is really above the
ground, whereas the aconite will thrust its
loop through the earth on one fine morning
and turn up its pretty yellow globe and green
frill the next almost like a conjuring trick.

A Mezereon has been in bloom for some
time, it is a small shrub with pinky lilac
blossoms, somewhat like those of the peach,
which are close to the stem, and come out
almost before the plant has finished shedding
its last year's leaves; the flowers have an
exquisite perfume. In the summer the stems
are covered with bright red berries which
look very pretty amidst the extremely neat
and dainty foliage. I have been told that
there is a white-flowered Mezereon which
is even still more beautiful, but I have not

been lucky enough either to see or possess
one. The *Pyrus Japonica* is also in bloom ;
this is a most aggravating shrub to gather
bloom from, the flowers invariably growing
in the most awkward places so that they
cannot be picked without greatly damaging
the whole shrub ; it is just one of those
beauties of the garden that must be seen
in situ to enjoy it properly ; seen thus, nothing exceeds the loveliness of its bright
cherry-red blossoms, golden anthers and pale
green leaflets, displayed on its picturesque
and straggling thorny branches.

I had some tubers of a sort of climbing nasturtium, *Tropeolum tuberosum*, given
me last spring, which I planted against a

wall; they grew and covered a large space
with pretty leaves and bright little flowers
of a decorative character. It is a native
of Peru, where, it is said, the tubers are
eaten. It is not quite hardy with us and
the tubers have to be taken up in the winter
and stored. When I went a week ago to
do this I found that each plant had formed
a huge mass of rather pretty looking tubers,
growing after the manner of potatoes, which I
have dried and put away. I thought I should
like to try what they tasted like, and so I
washed and boiled one or two. They boiled
soft and were of a yellowish colour inside,
with a strong aromatic and rather peculiar
flavour; not nice enough, however, to induce
me to cultivate them for the table.

LETTER XVIII

29th January, 1895.

DEAR MARCO — If "winter and rough
weather" are not the "only enemies" that
the countryman has to put up with they
are certainly the most important. A town-
dweller is not brought so continually face to
face with the wild forces of Nature, or ex-
periences such a succession of object lessons
on the weakness of man when opposed to the
baffling effects of those forces, as a countryman. It is one thing to sit over a cup of
coffee and a slice of toast in the breakfast
room of your snug town house and read

reports in the morning paper of floods, blizzards, and disastrous storms, but quite another to dwell in the very midst of the scenes of these disasters.

To wake up in the morning and see the sun rise over a huge lake which the day before was a broad meadow. To start for a walk and find yourself blocked, the footpath having entirely disappeared, or the water rushing over the road in a torrent, leaving its surface afterwards like so much shingle. To see small cottages with the stream running in at their front and out at their back doors, gaps torn out of their garden hedges, and the contents of their rubbish heaps carried away and scattered broadcast over the adjacent meadows, making them look, when the waters have subsided, like a field of battle. Or to find, after one such blizzard as we had last week, bushels of snow driven beneath your doors, or worse still through the cracks between the tiles of your roof, from whence it has to be caught in pails and bath-tubs

when it melts and comes through the bedroom ceilings.

. In the garden you may find one morning,
as I did lately, an old wall blown down by
the gale, covering with its *débris* a favourite
strawberry bed; or a large limb from a
walnut tree fallen on the tops of some
gooseberry bushes. Your work will be cut
out pretty well for you sometimes in relieving
evergreens and other things from the crushing
weight of snow with which they get laden.

As to keeping appointments with distant
neighbours, or taking your children to the
little festive gatherings to which they have
been invited, the difficulties of a moonless
night and deep snow in a state of thaw can
be readily imagined. A thunderstorm in
town makes a noise, and the deluge of rain,
which accompanies it, is inconvenient, but in
the country when you are told that six
bullocks have been struck dead by one flash
of lightning in a meadow at no great distance
from your house, or see a tree by the side of

a footpath which is your favourite Sunday
walk, burning internally, having been struck
the day before, a sense of the insecurity of
life, to which the town-dweller is a stranger,
naturally creeps over you. The wind is, however, always tempered to the shorn lamb, and
I must confess that there are many compensa-
tions for these discomforts of "winter and
rough weather."   Sunrise over a flooded
meadow is very beautiful.   Market people
crossing a flooded piece of road in waggons
or boats make a good subject for a picture.
Clean snow is a splendid thing for the children to play in, whilst the work of clearing
it away from the paths or off the laden boughs
is an invigorating and interesting occupation,
and remarkably good for one's liver.

The bad state of the roads often affords a
ready excuse for breaking an appointment to
which you may be indifferent.   As to that
wall that came down, I was greatly relieved
at finding that it was my neighbour who had
to pay for rebuilding it.

" The new soft fallen mask of snow" in
my shrubbery is pierced all over by the little
yellow globes of the winter aconites; they
looked very miserable until the snow came,
but now when the sun shines they seem

Bird's Winter   Feeding Board.

quite happy, each managing to keep a little
hollow around its stem and green frill, all
stretching their little heads as far as they
can to catch the sun. Feeding the birds
is now a constant care, they empty the little

storehouse on its long pole in no time, and
it has to be replenished several times a day.
All through the winter, during the coldest
nights, I hear the owls; the frost makes
them apparently extra clamorous, but what
they

" pit their painch in
I ain 'tis past my comprehension."

Surely no mice, beetles, or small birds would
be stirring in such weather.   The ground
must be as hard as iron, and where they can
find food I cannot imagine.   Birds of prey
can, I believe, fast longer than other birds,
and owls are at any rate very warmly
clothed.

I forgot to mention, as one of the effects
of the flood, that a heap of coke that was
piled in the kitchen garden got lifted by
the flood and floated about in every direction,
so that ever since small deposits of this useful
stuff keep turning up on the borders; coke
does not make a good top-dressing.

LETTER XIX

11th February, 1895.

DEAR MARCO—This prolonged frost is very trying. It is perhaps a little warmer to-day, but the wind is bitter and in the north-east still. Yesterday morning there was a strongly marked solar halo, and a fall in the barometer, but nothing came of it except a slight increase of wind.

In feeding the birds I have the greatest difficulty in preventing the sparrows, rooks, and starlings from getting pretty nearly all I put out. The thrushes and blackbirds

fare very badly; the thrushes will persist
in keeping on the ground, they do not alight
on to the feeding board but creep about and,
as it were, "stalk" their food stealthily and
deliberately; in consequence of which the
other more alert birds snatch it away from
under their very beaks.   As to the black-

Thrush in Cold Weather.

birds, they waste the best part of their time
in fighting and chasing away each other
and the smaller birds.   I am quite at a loss
to know how to manage the stuff so that
these two sorts should get their proper share.
The thrushes look by far the most miserable
of any of the birds, with their feathers all

puffed up, quite unlike the slim and gallant
shape they present in the summer. The
blackbirds, on the other hand, never seem
to lose the pride they take in the gallantry
of their appearance, and raise and lower
their tails on alighting as usual. I provide
for the thrushes a little at times, by hunting
out lumps of hybernating snails which I
throw on to the lawns, where the thrushes
soon make quick work in despatching
them. I have never noticed any other bird
but the thrush attack these snails.

The tits do not really need much outdoor
relief, as the trees, bushes, old walls, &c., which
are their usual hunting grounds, are not inter-
fered with by the frost or snow. They never
appear to me in the least distressed by the
cold as other birds do, and I only hang bones
and fat on strings for them, partly to keep
them away from my gooseberry bushes, but
chiefly for the pleasure of seeing them close
up to my window. The little brown wrens
never seem to come for food at all; no

doubt they likewise are not much inconvenienced by the frost.   I see many creeping and flitting about, under the ivy and along the ledges of the old walls in the garden, looking quite happy and well.

The moorhens have not come up for food this year as they did during other winters. The reason of which is, I think, that they have plenty of snugly covered runs beside the river this year, which supply them with the necessary food and shelter.   These runs are occasioned by the fact of the river having been very high when the frost began, and of its having fallen gradually ever since ; this has caused the formation of huge flakes of ice in tiers, one above another, along the banks ; on the tops of these layers of ice the snow drifted, whilst the water fell from beneath, leaving long sheltered arcades, the ground on the floors of which is probably unfrozen. These arcades have little openings into them here and there, through which the moorhens no doubt pass, finding inside most congenial cover and feeding places. In most other winters, since I have lived here, the river was low when the frost began, so that the banks became hard and frostbound at once; in those winters the moorhens came much into my kitchen garden and frequently on to the lawn, even close up to the house, after the food we threw out.

The river has not been frozen right across here during this long frost, neither has the ice at the edges been of sufficient strength for skating on, no doubt owing to the constant fall of the water. Above the weir at Benson, where the water is penned up and still, however, some very strong ice has formed, on which plenty of skating has been carried on.

The flocks of gulls, which I hear have visited London owing to the long protracted frost, have not, as far as I know, been seen on the upper reaches of the Thames, though I have seen a solitary gull or two occasionally pass by.

I was much astonished to discover this morning that a clump of daffodils, which are

L

planted on the edge of the lawn, had pierced the turf and were showing quite three inches of green leaves above the ground ; the sun had just cleared the snow from the ground where they were, snow which had been lying there for nearly a fortnight, but the ground itself was still as hard as iron. How they possibly managed to force their way up I cannot imagine. I am quite sure that they have somehow come through since the long frost began, because during the mild weather that preceded it, I had expected to see them, and had searched for them in vain every day. These daffodils grow on rather a sheltered bank by the edge of the grass, and have not had a very deep covering of snow on them at any time, but the ground was and is still frozen hard and deeply around them.

I have not troubled you with statistics or thermometer readings anent the frost, as you get these, *ad nauseam*, in the daily papers. I have no thermometer in the garden, except a sort of living one, a certain aucuba laurel, which grows just outside our garden door; it is one of the plain green aucubas, a male plant I believe; it is very sensitive to cold and has its regular degrees of misery marked on its foliage during the cold weather in the most unmistakable manner. So long as the frost keeps off its leaves splay out, large, green, and healthy, a slight frost causes them to droop, a harder one to curl inwards longitudinally, whilst a severe one darkens and shrivels them in an alarming manner. They recover themselves as the frost gives in an exactly reverse order, and when the thaw is complete they once more stretch out green and healthy. I have become quite an expert at reading this thermometer, and for my purposes scarcely need another. I just open the back door, look at the state of the foliage before going to bed, and from it know quite well whether to put lamps to my water-pipes or not. It is a far easier, quicker, and nearly as effectual a way of finding out the temperature as to stand fiddling in the cold with a match, your spectacles, and a thermometer.

I do not take much interest in tables, records, or statistics, useful as they are no doubt in their way ; all I want to do is to save my plants and my pipes, and know how many blankets to put over me in bed.

Painting in my studio just now is almost out of the question, for in spite of a large Gill stove I cannot keep my hands warm for five consecutive minutes. I just look at my picture, put on an occasional touch, and run away.

Though you do not care much for dogs, I know you love cats, and it would please you to see our brown Ben and a fluffy black kitten, named " The Royal Imp," play together. She does his toilet for him at times, in front of the fire, which he greatly enjoys ; on the other hand, when he licks her he makes her hair uncomfortably wet. A cat's tongue always feels rather dry and rough, and acts like a comb on the fur, but the dog's tongue is soft and wet.

LETTER XX

11th April, 1895.

DEAR MARCO—The remarkable winter
through which we have lately passed, has
necessarily been followed by an unusually
backward spring. The trees are only just
beginning to show signs of life ; the horse-
chestnut trees and one or two others are at
length bursting into bud, but the great
majority look much the same as they did at
Christmas time.

The most remarkable feature of the past
winter's frost was its extreme protraction.
Beginning with the New Year it continued,

with scarcely one break of importance, right up to the 18th of February, and even then did not end, as the severe frosts which Gilbert White described did, abruptly, with a sudden thaw, but took more than a fortnight before it could be said to have completely passed away ; thawing by day with the sunshine, and freezing again during the nights.

I found the ground had been so deeply penetrated by the frost that it was quite impossible to dig, even on the 6th of March, sufficiently to sow potatoes, and even a fortnight after that I found the interior of a heap of rotten leaves quite hard and caked with frost. It was more like a North German winter than an English one, the deep penetration of the frost being no doubt due to its extreme protraction. The havoc it played with the water-pipes in town will cause it to be remembered by Londoners for many years.

I am gradually becoming aware of my

various losses in the garden, some are irreparable, whilst others may, I hope, prove only partial. A lovely Maréchal Niel is very badly injured, I cannot see a sign of a bud on it at present, whereas, I have seen it in former years with large flower buds showing at this date. My China or monthly roses, on either side of the trellised path, are also seriously damaged; there is far more dead wood on them than living, with hardly any flower buds at all showing anywhere. These roses I have always accounted as most hardy, but they have proved themselves inferior in this respect to the damask, the cabbage, the maiden's blush or the sweet brier, all which seem none the worse for the frost. The *Rosa rugosa*, Austrian briar, and some of the hybrid perpetuals are also fairly well.

My rosemary bushes have been severely punished, one or two are quite dead and the others only just alive. The laurestines and some other evergreens are badly scorched, even the lavender looks snubbed and disheartened, but I think most of these things will revive and sprout afresh.

On the whole, thanks to the principle of having only hardy subjects in my garden, less damage has been done than I should have expected. The crocuses and scillas, though very late, were excessively beautiful this year. I had, through the kindness of my friend Miss Jekyll, the delight of seeing several large patches of Puschinias in bloom for the first time; they are bulbs with much resemblance of character to the *Scilla sibirica* but the flowers are of a delicate white with little longitudinal stripes of blue, or rather blue mingled with violet and green; they have also rather more flowers on each stem than the scillas. Miss Jekyll also gave me last autumn several other new good things, all of which are, I am happy to say, thriving; amongst others a dwarf Hemerocalis or day-lily, and a white sea-holly, *Eryngium giganteum*. I am afraid my *Iris Susiana* will not bloom this year, as it was impossible to

keep the cold out of the little greenhouse
for so long a period.

My alstrœmerias, of which I am very
proud, are pushing through the ground as
vigorously as ever, though the beds in which
they grow were, first of all, for a week or
more three feet under the flood-water, and
after that, in the winter, frozen nearly solid
for a month at least.   These Peruvian lilies,
as they are sometimes called, are generally
supposed to be rather delicate and tender,
but I am now convinced that, provided they
are let alone, they will survive any weather.
They must, however, be grown from seed,
doing best with me when self-sown.   Most
people try to establish them from seedlings,
which they buy in pots, but alstrœmerias
scarcely ever succeed in this way, the fact
being that they will not stand transplanting,
for their roots are long and hair-like, and the
least damage to these injures the plant fatally.
These plants just suit my " let things alone "
style of gardening and thrive amazingly,

their wonderfully showy blooms being in
the summer one of the chief glories of my
garden.

The birds seem very well and much
sweet singing goes on, though I think that
there are hardly so many thrushes and blackbirds as usual. The rooks' nests suffered
much damage during the gale on the 24th of
March.

I am greatly puzzled about the ants, how
it is that they survive in their nests through
the floods and frosts. We have many ant-
nests along the brickwork by the edge of
the river, mostly of the common black ant,
which must have been under, at least, six
feet of water, for a fortnight during the great
flood; and more or less waterlogged afterwards for a much longer time; they then
passed through the late severe winter, have
since been flooded again slightly, and yet
to-day I saw the usual little streams of ants
running to and fro along the bricks just as
usual. Are their nests watertight? Do

they hybernate? And if so, how are they protected from water and frost combined? Is it possible that they manage to close up their nests so that the water cannot penetrate? If they do this how do they obtain air? I have often noticed how difficult it is to wet an ant, or to drown one; perhaps they are covered with some oily substance which keeps them dry, and they may perhaps keep their nests dry by the same oily substance; but still they would have no air when under water. I would look the subject up in books, but I feel sure this is just one of those things that books would say nothing about. I sat next Sir John Lubbock last year at the Academy dinner, I wish I had thought of it then as I might have asked him.

LETTER XXI

30th May, 1895.

DEAR MARCO—The following account of
the strange behaviour of a small bird will no
doubt interest you.   At Mr. H. W. Wells's
house, Whitecross, which is half a mile from
Riverside, about three weeks ago, a wagtail
took to a persistent habit of flying up to one
of the upper windows and tapping repeatedly
and loudly with its beak against the glass.
The room to which this window belonged
was a nursery, and you may judge of the

character and persistency of the bird's tapping, for it became quite a nuisance, waking
up the children out of their midday sleep.
The bird came always at the same time,
perched on the sill, and flew up repeatedly,
a dozen or more times consecutively, striking
its beak loudly on the glass each time.   All
manner of contrivances were tried, in the
shape of strings and cotton to keep the bird
away, but with no effect ; some rat-gins were
even set on the sill where the bird perched,
but I am happy to say it simply avoided them.
After a bit the tappings became less frequent,
and although the bird still pays an occasional
visit it no longer occasions annoyance.

It seems almost impossible to account
for this bird's strange behaviour.   There
were no flies or spiders apparent on the
outsides or insides of the window panes.
It was to the night nursery window only
the bird came ; if the bird had been attracted
by its own reflection in the glass, there were
several other windows on that side of the

house, the west, in which the reflection would have been seen equally well but to which it never went.

Another little bird puzzle has occupied my mind lately, which is, that throughout the hot dry weather we have had for the last fortnight, a pair of rooks have taken to feeding on the lawn, just beneath the sycamore tree, every morning for an hour or two. I am quite sure it is the same pair, as I have looked at them very carefully ; they walk about always over the same spot, pecking at the ground much as the starlings do. I call it the same *spot*, as the area over which they walk is very limited. The puzzle to me is what they find to eat. The grass just there is almost brown with the drought, the only living things on it that I can discover being a few ants and some earwigs ; but there are many more of these insects on other parts of the lawn to which the rooks do not seem to go. And why have these rooks deserted their companions, unless they have been ostracised by them for some breach of etiquette in rook life? They are unmistakably rooks, and are rather tame, allowing me to approach quite near at times. I wish there was some ornithological " Sherlock Holmes " to whom one might apply for a solution of these and other bird mysteries.

The drought this spring is nearly as bad as that which occurred the year before last, and the outlook for gardeners and farmers is becoming very serious. It is true we have had a few showers, just to break the long spell, but as the reports in the papers show, the precipitation, as they term it, has been very deficient ever since the commencement of the year.

It is strange that all the different sorts of weather have come to us in lumps lately ; long rains and floods in the autumn—long frosts in the winter, and long drought in the spring. The long frost and the long drought have both been accompanied by a persistent strong wind from the north and east.

I have, by dint of watering from the river,

kept my flower borders in wonderful beauty :
I take my coat off and do it myself; I cannot
trust the gardener, for he *will* use a huge can,
with a great fierce rose on it, which sends a
miniature thunder shower on to the tops of
the plants, thereby battering them to the
ground, whilst the water runs off in streams
without penetrating to the roots at all.   I have
two handy-sized cans with long noses and no
roses on them ; with these I give each plant
that really wants it, once a week, a whole
can all to itself, right close down to the
ground, where the roots are, allowing plenty
of time for it to soak well in.   Of course this
takes time, but it is the only way, and the
result more than repays the trouble taken.

One of my borders is just now in great
perfection, for in it are masses of irises and
pæonies of various shades of colour, oriental
poppies, large deep-red lilies (*Davuricum*),
monks' hoods, and doronicums, these form the
heavy brigade of the border ; a variety of
smaller and perhaps more interesting things

mixed in front of these, and in the front of
all masses of what are termed carpeting
plants. This whole bed is raised, from the
level of the tennis court, about three feet
high ; its front is kept up, for its entire length,
by a red brick wall, so that as you stand
beside it you have all the plants and flowers
in the border raised up, and their beauties
displayed like goods upon a linendraper's
counter. Flowers gain much by this arrangement, you have not to stoop to look at them,
and the bare spaces of mould (if there are
any) do not catch the eye, owing to the angle
at which the view is taken. It is most con-
venient too for weeding and picking, as
stooping is dispensed with. I sometimes
think if I had to form a new flower garden
that I would have all the beds raised up thus,
with small retaining walls, say three feet high,
with the paths sunk between them. It might
be made very pretty, with occasional arches
over the paths and steps up and down in
places. From a distance it would look all

M

flowers, the paths being out of sight. You
can have no idea, without having seen it,
how much flowers gain by being raised up
thus, nearer to the level of the eye. At any
rate I think that a large part of every garden
should be treated in this fashion. I remember E. W. Cooke, R.A., had something
of the sort in his garden at Groombridge,
which he used to call "The Bamboozleum,"
the paths were scooped out amongst and
between some sandstone rocks, the hollows
were planted with bamboos, and the raised
ledges with Alpine plants ; it was a delightful
spot. In greenhouses and conservatories
flowers are seen thus raised up, but the pots
and obvious artificiality detract from the
effect.

The floods last November came across the
tennis-court right up to this raised border, and
completely covered a little bog-garden which
is just beneath the wall, and the whole of
this small bog-garden must afterwards have
been frozen solid for a long time in the

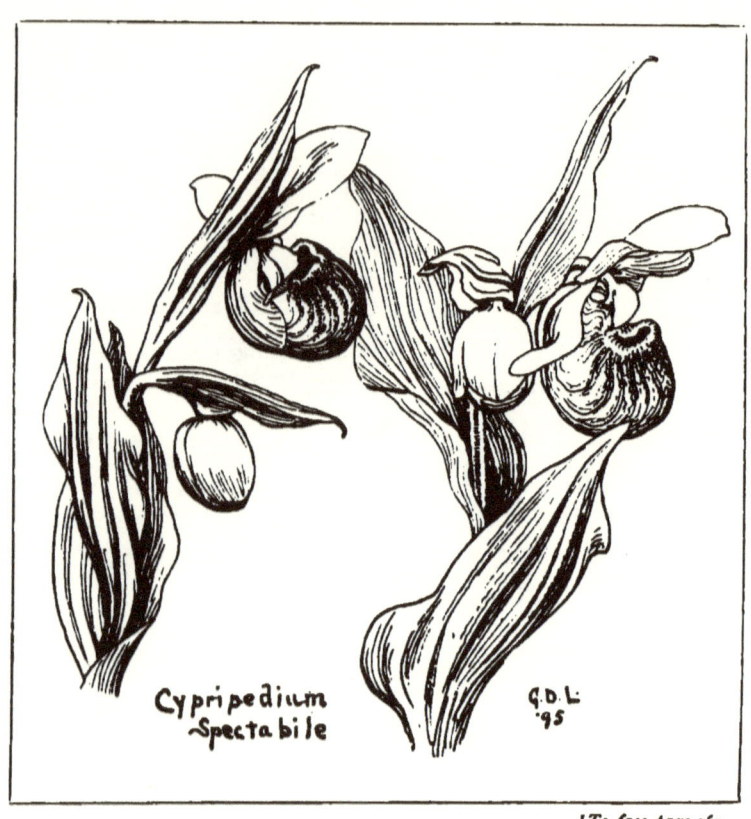

Cypripedium
Spectabile

G.D.L.
'95

[*To face page* 163.

winter, and yet in spite of all this a beautiful orchid, *Cypripedium spectabile*, is now more vigorous and flourishing than ever, each stem having two large creamy white buds ready to burst upon it. I have had the roots of this plant for three years, and this is the first bloom it has shown ; you can easily imagine my excitement. A buck-bean in this bog has also done wonderfully well, blooming luxuriantly. Here also are some epimediums, the foliage of which is very delicate and graceful, they have wiry stalks, like the maiden-hair fern, with leaves of exquisite shape and lovely colour. At the four corners of this little garden are clumps of Japan irises, all very rich in promise of bloom. These semi-aquatic plants, though they possess the frail beauty of hot-house subjects, are all really as hardy as groundsel ; these of mine having been left alone, unsheltered in any way, during the floods and frosts, have come out unscathed and lovely. I must say, however, that a frost in the

middle or at the end of May, will do them
much harm, though only of a temporary
character; also that the whole little bog has
to be enclosed with wire, or the blackbirds
and thrushes would during the dry, hot,
weather, very soon scratch the place to
pieces. Some frogs have taken up their
abode in it, and keep it free from ants, which
might otherwise become troublesome.

Just before I intended to post this letter, I
witnessed, this afternoon, a bird's action,
about which I had often heard and read, but
never seen. It was that of a nuthatch cracking a nut. It has been often described
accurately and fully, but I thought you might
like to hear my account, taken fresh from
nature. In the kitchen garden there is a
large weeping willow hanging over the river,
near which at sundry times I have heard
a tapping noise, but never could find out what
caused it. I did not expect to see a nuthatch
there, as, most usually, I see these birds on
the sycamore or walnut-tree at the other

[To face page 165.

NUTHATCH AND NUT.

end of the garden.   This afternoon, as I was
dipping water from the river beneath the
willow, I heard the noise just over my head,
I stepped back gently, and there, very close
indeed, on the slanting trunk of the tree, I
saw the bird and its nut as plainly as possible.
The willow bark is deeply corrugated with
narrow furrows, into the angle of one of
which the bird had thrust the nut (one of our
filberts) and was perched above it, holding on
firmly by its claws.   It drew itself up, almost
to a slope backwards, and with rigid body
and neck came down on the nut with its
beak, with machine-like accuracy.   I made a
roughish sketch which I enclose.   Every
now and then it would go round and give a
tap or two from below, apparently for the
purpose of the adjustment of the nut; but
the main work was done from above.   The
bird remained some time, whilst I was there,
hard at work, but flew away at last, leaving
its nut unfinished.

Two things I derived from this observation,

first that the bird had chosen this tree on account of the character of its bark and of its sloping trunk, which made the retention of the nut in its place an easy matter ; and secondly, that as this was the 30th of May the nut must have come from a store, probably hidden somewhere by the bird, for of course the nut must have been a last year's nut : as I have heard this tapping at different times all through the winter and spring the store of nuts must have been pretty large to have lasted until now.

LETTER XXII

11th June, 1895.

DEAR MARCO—When visiting our annual
exhibitions I have often been rather distressed
at the carelessness, as to the facts of nature,
displayed by many artists in the introduction
of flowers into their pictures. For instance,
water-lilies are frequently represented growing
in what is obviously meant to be shallow
water ; whereas they grow only in deep water,
and where the bottom is soft and muddy.
White water-lilies are constantly painted with
the foliage of the common yellow one ; the

leaves of the white water-lily are smaller than those of the yellow, and have a purplish-red hue.   The common purple German iris is repeatedly introduced as an aquatic plant, growing in any sort of water at any sort of depth.   I have seen even the yellow water flag figuring in a picture in very much deeper water than I believe it possibly could grow, represented, in fact, in the *middle* of a wide pool or river amongst *reeds*, which mostly indicate quite deep water ; the yellow flag, as far as I know, only grows on the margins of the water, and is seldom found more than half submerged.   In one picture I noticed roses, poppies, and Roman hyacinths in bloom together ; in many others the relative sizes and proportions of the flowers introduced were quite curiously erroneous.   Frequent liberties are taken with the colour of the foliage of laurels and other shrubs when introduced in back-grounds, a cold bluish green is used when it should have been a deep rich olive, and *vice versâ*.

I have seen the teasel, fearfully scamped
and libelled, even to representing it with grace-
fully curved stems.   If any plant is precise,
straight, and symmetrical it is the teasel ;
surely if a graceful, curling line is wanted
there are numbers of plants which would
have served the purpose.

Then again, one sees quite modern bred
roses introduced into pictures the subjects of
which are taken from classic or mediæval
periods.

This violation of the facts and truths of
nature is not confined alone to the representation of flowers, but is often displayed in
other ways.

I noticed in a landscape this year a windmill going merrily round with one wind, whilst
the clouds and some trees were evidently
blown by quite another.   It would do no
harm to our painters if those who reviewed
their works in the papers had sufficient inti-
macy with the ordinary truths of nature to
be able to detect, at times, these misrepresen-

tations.   Our greatest modern critic, who,
alas, no longer writes, would never have
passed over or tolerated such slovenly inac-
curacies.

I must say, however, that many of our
landscape painters display the greatest love
and veneration for natural truth.   Alfred
Parsons and Ernest Waterlow, for example,
being at all times thoroughly conscientious
and trustworthy in their representations of
nature.   I think Waterlow's pair of pictures
in No. VIII. room this year quite perfect in
their truthfulness and beauty.

I send you a few more studies of seed pods
which I have lately made.   This one is that
of a winter aconite, which I came across the
other day ; I had never noticed the seed case
of this little favourite of mine before and was
greatly struck by its quaintness and beauty,
either when viewed from above or from the
side : the picturesque little frill which shields
the flower as it emerges from the ground at
its birth remains faithful even unto death.   A

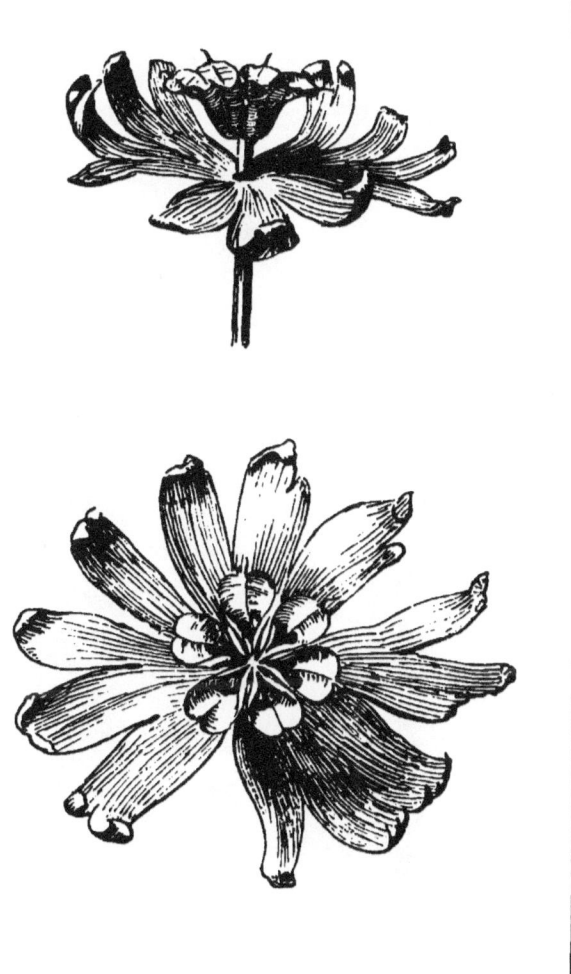

[*To face page* 170.

SEED-CASE OF WINTER ACONITE.

:

similar faithfulness is displayed by the petals
of the Christmas rose, they lose their lovely
whiteness it is true, but remain in a leathery
hard state around the cluster of seed
pods to the very end. These seed pods

Helleborus niger   Helleborus viridis

look in my drawing rather like little sucking
pigs at their meals; their shape is rendered
perhaps more intelligible in the seed head of
the green hellebore, where they look un-
commonly like short stout pea pods. The
green hellebore is a native of our country; my

root came from Bagley Wood, Oxford. The crown-imperial seed case speaks for itself, so like a knight's mace ; to show the projecting

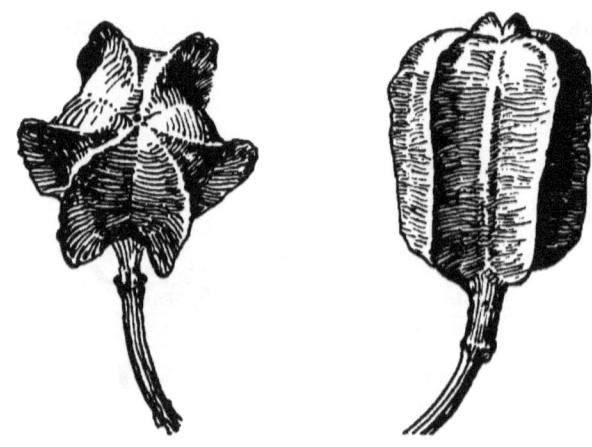

Crown-imperial

flanges better I have drawn it from above as well as in elevation.

And here are some seed heads of the common wood hyacinth or bluebell; they have a lot of picturesque drawing in them. The three-fold shape, so characteristic of all the lily tribe, is beautifully marked. These hyacinths sow themselves very freely,

many of my borders are quite pestered with
their young seedlings. The little Siberian
scilla also sows itself freely,
but the seedlings do not
spread so far and wide as
do those of the common
bluebell; this is chiefly
owing to the different character of the stalks which
support the seed cases of
the two plants. The pod
of *Scilla Siberica* is large
and heavy, and its stalk is
weak and thin, so that the
pod when ripe lies on the
ground and sheds its seed
close to the parent bulb.
The seed cases of the wood
hyacinth, on the contrary, are
supported on a tall stiff stalk

Wood hyacinth

which rises well above the decaying foliage.
The foliage itself, as it dies, falls over and
forms a sort of circular inclined plane around

the stalk, on which the seeds, when they fall,
roll down in every direction to the ground.
This circular inclined plane is often very

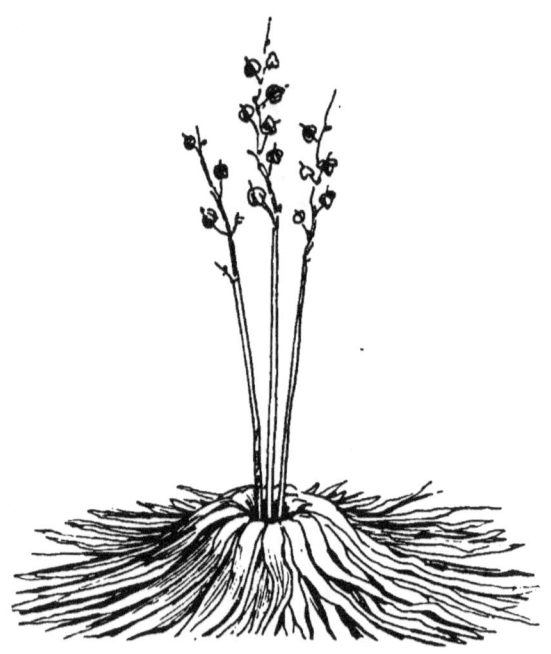

Wood hyacinth run to seed

wide, so that the seeds are scattered to a
distance from the parent bulb, and so the plant
spreads and spreads until our woods and
coppices are blue with the pretty flowers.

We are again experiencing a severe
drought; and its effects are very serious
to the farmers around here, where sheep-
farming is one of the chief industries. The
flocks depend largely on roots for their food
in winter, and I have been told that unless
we get some copious showers during the next
fortnight the root crop will be entirely ruined,
so you can imagine how anxiously the rain is
longed for.

The long continued prevalence of northerly
winds which has characterised the last six or
seven years is very remarkable, and I cannot
help associating it in some way with that
peculiar white glare which has been so seldom absent from the sun during this period.
This glare is seen, when there are no clouds
about, pervading the sky, in the neighbourhood of the sun, most conspicuously in the
mornings and evenings. I have pointed it
out to friends here frequently, and am astonished that little or no notice is taken of
it by those expert in meteorological matters.

As far as I have noticed this glare, it is rather more conspicuous when one of these spells of north wind sets in. These winds die away at night, when the sky is generally clear, and the thermometer low. In the mornings the sky is clear and there is no wind, but just as the sun gains power, about nine o'clock, the wind begins to blow with great force, sometimes bringing up clouds with it but very often blowing all day long with a clear sky. The drying up effect of the wind and sun together, with the coldness at night, have a most disastrous effect on all vegetable growth.

LETTER XXIII

18th June, 1895.

DEAR MARCO—A few days ago, on a walk with my wife and some friends through the meadows, we came to a gate that was secured by a chain in which was what is called "A Shepherd's Link." To all appearances there was no possibility of undoing this chain unless this link could be opened. To save the ladies from having to climb the gate we tried in every possible way to solve the mystery of the fastening, but without success. On our return I was determined to have another try, and,

N

after some time, succeeded. The little
secret was simple enough but extremely
ingenious. I have drawn you a " Shepherd's
Link" but do not intend to explain how it
can be opened. The link is almost exactly
like an ordinary chain swivel; its two parts
move freely one within the other, but both
are quite solid and simple in construction.

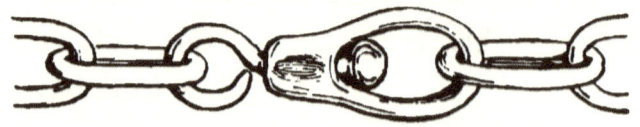

No force is required, and I have little doubt
but that a shepherd could open it in a
moment, even in the dark. I have repeatedly
seen these links securing gate-chains in the
country, and have climbed over without
stopping to examine the fastenings, taking
them for some sort of simple padlock which
required a key.

Lilies have rather curious ways with them
sometimes. Occasionally the bulbs will re-

main dormant in the ground for a whole
season, springing up and flourishing the
next year apparently all the stronger for
their rest. About five years ago I planted
two bulbs of a lily called *Pomponium
verum*, which has pretty scarlet Turk's cap
flowers ; they flowered meagrely the first
summer after planting ; the next year they
sent up plenty of foliage but very few blooms ;
the year after that they seemed to be in a
very poor way indeed, and they never came
up at all on the fourth year. Now, this year,
there are three fine flowering spikes with
one or two off-sets, all very vigorous and
strong. A puzzling thing about these lilies is,
that they have not come up in the place where
they were originally planted ; I put them
in the very centre of the bed and now they
are some at one edge and some at another.
I am quite sure that the bed has not been
disturbed by spade, trowel, or fork, and am at
a loss to account for the apparent movement
of the bulbs. Other bulbs are in this bed

beside the lilies — crocuses, scillas, and some
Spanish irises ; there are, too, some Iceland
poppies ; possibly the lilies have been crowded
to one side by the growth around them.

We went over to Bradfield College last
Thursday, to see the Greek play *Alcestis*.
No doubt you have read about these per-
formances, which are given entirely in the
open air in a well-constructed amphitheatre.
The proscenium and all the accessories are
designed with the utmost care and taste, the
classic effect of the whole being very striking.
All the while the performance was going on,
when we were there, there was a lovely blue
sky overhead, and sweet birds were singing
amidst the wild rose-bushes and clematis,
birch, ash, and walnut-trees, with which the
summit of the amphitheatre is surrounded.
In the centre of the semicircular pavement is
an altar, on which incense is kept burning.
The dresses of the actors and chorus are
admirably designed and the colours most harmonious.   The acting is animated and free

from conventionality. The female parts are taken by boys, skilfully made up. The musicians have quaint lyres and flutes. The chorus of old men sing their strophes and antistrophes to a droning air, moving in a slow measure all the time around the altar. All legs and arms are *really* bare, and the sandals are no made up things from the costumier's, but genuine ones which make a strange clattering when any quick movement takes place. I wished much you could have been there, as I feel sure you would have enjoyed it. Tadema was there on Saturday and was greatly delighted. This pretty revival is almost entirely due to the energy of the present Warden, who himself acted the principal part of King Admetus.

On Sunday night we were favoured by a visit from a young brown owl. My daughter noticed the bird first, as it was sitting on one of the window ledges on the side of our house which is next the road. We all went out to look at it ; there was plenty of light still, as it was but nine o'clock and the 16th of June. The bird seemed very tame and flew down on to the portico over the front door, then up on to the hood of a water-pipe, which was close to the window of the bath-

room. I went up there, opened the window, and looked out at the bird, which was scarcely three feet off; it did not fly away, but gave a juvenile " Tu-whee," and stared earnestly at my spectacles. I had a comfortable look at the bird, its soft plumage and large eyes being very engaging. I made a sort of imitation of an owl's hoot, and the bird answered me in his own way directly. It remained about the house for some time, appearing at different windows. Country people have stupid prejudices against these birds, accounting them of ill omen ; for my own part I am so fond of their quaintness and exquisite plumage, to say nothing of the good they do, that I only look upon such a visit as this as a thing to be remembered thankfully.

This bird was, no doubt, a young one that had but just commenced to fly. Several pairs of brown owls nest near our house. My neighbour tells me that they have lately taken to building in the old elms in his garden. We also see owls in the sycamore tree, though I do not think that there are any nests. When an owl flies very close to any one the two things which startle most are the size of the head and broad wings of the bird, and the absolute noiselessness of its flight.

LETTER XXIV

9th July, 1895.

DEAR MARCO—The fascination which running water has for me is, I believe, inherited
from my father. The love of water as a
means of recreation, is strongly felt not only
by myself and my children, but by my brothers
and their children as well.

My brother Bradford and I, as boys, were
never happier than when engaged in making
little dams and waterfalls across some small
brook or other ; no walk much pleased us that
did not lead either to or past some stream or
river. Sailing boats and the sea are, as you

know, my eldest brother Robert's chief delight. My own children seem never tired of playing (messing ?) about on the edge of the river ; they care little for fishing compared to the delight of making little harbours, canals, &c., in the gravelly beach which is exposed when the river is low in summer time. Most of our family possess, too, a natural ability for mechanical science ; we are all, as the Americans would say, "tinkers," a talent no doubt derived from my grandfather, who was distinctly a genius in this respect.

I have a sketch which my father made from recollection, of the happy days he spent as a boy in Chester county with his Uncle Ward, who had a farm and mill on a tributary of the Brandywine Creek, which proves that he had just this same delight in running water. His cousin had fixed for him, on a small stream, a little water-wheel with cams attached to its axle, which acted on two wooden hammers, causing them to rise and fall on little

anvils as the wheel went round and round
with the water.

My father used to describe the delight that
he took in this water-wheel, the pleasure he
felt in watching it, and in paddling all day
long barefoot about the brook. I have made
a rough copy of his sketch for you, in the
background is his uncle's log house.

My father told many stories of the happy
times he spent with this uncle Ward; amongst
others I recollect one about a turkey cock
who suffered in his old age from mental
aberration, which took this comic form of
showing itself. It one day scratched a large
hole beneath an apple tree, and having rolled
a number of apples into it, quietly settled
itself down on them and sat there for days
with the evident purpose of hatching them:
nothing would persuade it to relinquish its self-
imposed task until the apples all went rotten.

I heard a rather amusing story of a spaniel
that belongs to a farmer living not far
from here. The kennel of this dog is situ-

THE BOYHOOD OF C. R. LESLIE, R.A.

[To face page 186.

ated in an orchard which is much frequented by poultry. In the mornings the spaniel lies outside his kennel—he always maintains a very friendly manner with the cocks and hens—and occasionally a hen will enter his kennel and there lay an egg. The dog never disturbs a hen who is thus occupied, but after she has layed her egg, finished her noise, and gone away, he enters the kennel and gobbles up the egg.

Just now the ants in my garden are very busy bringing up their eggs in piles to the surface of the ground, in order, as I suppose, that the sun's rays may warm and hatch them. Once or twice I have uncovered one of these subterranean piles, and taken all the eggs I could carry on a trowel and thrown them into the river. After which I have poured a can of cold water upon the place in order to drive the ants away by flooding the nest, but even after all this drastic treatment I have invariably found on visiting the spot that, in the course of a day or two, all the damage seems to have been repaired and a fresh lot of eggs again heaped on the surface.

I have treated one nest in this way three times and yet to-day the ants are again placing a fresh pile of eggs on the top. From which I gather that though their perseverance and their fecundity are enormous their reasoning powers are very deficient.

It is this perpetual bringing up of the eggs to hatch in the warmth of the sun, which occasions the ant-hills in the meadows, for fine grains of earth are brought up each time, with the eggs, gradually forming large heaps.

After a heavy rain in summer time, a number of small ant-heaps are always seen on different parts of the lawn. Are these little heaps the proceeds of the repairs which have become necessary after the rain? If you examine these small piles you will generally find that they contain a few eggs. Have these been brought up to dry? Or if the heap were left alone would it in a short time become larger and contain more eggs? I am disposed to believe it would, but how is it that this bringing up of eggs always first commences after a heavy rain? I never see any such little heaps on the lawn during a long dry hot spell of weather. The ants on the lawn all seem to be small red ones of the same sort as are found in meadows, in which, when the grass is cut, quite large ant-heaps are frequently laid open by the scythe, which operation discomforts the little red ants and blunts the scythe badly.

After a field has been mown starlings and other birds flock to it, so I expect that these dismantled heaps are part of the attraction.

LETTER XXV

6th August, 1895.

DEAR MARCO—I was up in town last week
and the week before, strange to say, staying
at my old house in the Grove End Road. I
went there to paint the portrait of a little
granddaughter of Sir William Agnew. It was
curious that I should be thus painting in my
old studio, which I built, but which is no
longer mine. In the afternoons I sometimes
walked about the well-remembered neigh-

bourhood, in which I was born, and where
you and I passed so many happy years
with the " Boys of the Old St. John's
Wood Brigade," now, alas! sadly diminished
in number.   Many changes have taken
place, none perhaps more striking than the
entire demolition of No. 18, St. John's
Wood Road, Sir Edwin Landseer's house.
The boundary walls of the garden were
still up, but doomed; they were covered,
it being the election time, with posters of
the rival candidates for Marylebone.   A
few trees still stood in the garden, but of
the house itself not one stone was left.   In
its place, already huge blocks of artisans'
dwellings were rising, every available space
being piled up with bricks and building
materials.

I knew Sir Edwin all my life, and when I
came to live in Grove End Road used to see
him continually.   In those days he suffered
much from depression of mind, and when
pressed in his work would send round for me

to come and help him, in some small way, with his pictures. I used to paint accessories for him, such as the checks on a Tartan shawl, or other objects of still life. Once I painted a hand holding a horse's bridle, Sir Edwin himself standing as my model. I put in also the yellow water-lilies in his picture of the *Fight between the Eagles and Swans.* Landseer always went over my work afterwards, with a big brush, to prevent its looking too neat and finished. He generally persuaded me to stay and lunch with him, after which he would sometimes go out with me, take a hansom, and drive all round Hampstead or Highgate to cheer and freshen himself up. He could not bear, at these times of depression, to be left alone, and I frequently stayed and dined with him, after which we played at billiards or went to the theatre. T. H. Hills,—"Dear Hills" as he was always called—was Landseer's greatest friend at that time ; he looked after all his business affairs for him and did everything for his health and comfort that his kind heart could possibly think of: Landseer loved him deeply, clinging to him as a nervous child does to its mother.

Landseer had an old servant, his butler, valet and faithful slave, named William, who knew and understood his master's ways and habits perfectly. Though Sir Edwin would bully this man at times, when he was put out, he thoroughly appreciated his usefulness and could not have got on at all without him. William was particularly assiduous in guarding the outer portal; no one could by any possibility gain direct access to Sir Edwin; not even though an appointment had been made. The answer would invariably be, " Sir Hedwin is not at home."   H.R.H. the Prince Consort himself once received this answer when he called, amplified on that occasion by the assurance that " he had gone to a wedding," an entire fiction on William's part, as the Prince found out, for on walking boldly in and round the garden he noticed

Sir Edwin looking out of his studio window.

I paid so little regard to William's customary formula that at last he gave it up and would merely show me into the drawing-room and say that he would go and tell Miss Jessy. I had seldom long to wait before Landseer himself would appear, in an old home-spun shooting jacket ; calico sleeves were tied on his arms like those that butchers' wear. He wore generally an old straw hat, the brim of which was lined with green, had his palette and brushes in his hand and looked extremely picturesque, reminding me strongly of some of the figures in Rembrandt's etchings. He did not, at once, speak, but would gaze at me with a queer scrutinising look, full of expression, for a moment or two, his lips beginning to quiver and move a little before the words came. He was always extremely kind and courteous in his manner. I was often struck by the great deference and politeness which he invariably showed to any

woman, whether a lady or not ; in short, his
manners were those of a well-bred English
gentleman.

Of his brilliance in society in general I
have no need to tell, but it may be interesting
to know that he was equally polished and
amusing at his own table, though at it, besides
himself, sat only his sister, one of his brothers,
or some humble individual like myself.   He
was devotedly fond of his sister Jessy, and
well he might be, for sure never man had a
sister more self-sacrificing and affectionate.

The garden was very large and extended
around the house on three of its sides ; it had
been carefully planted with trees by Sir
E. so as to shut out as many indications
of other houses as possible.   It reached from
the St. John's Wood Road right to the canal,
just where it issues from the Aberdeen Place
tunnel.   A well-grown silver birch grew in
one part, which Landseer said he had brought
from the Highlands as a seedling.   There
was also a fine old mulberry tree.

' The original house when Landseer first
came to live in St. John's Wood was quite a
small cottage, rustic in character; I have seen
a sketch in water-colours of it done by Miss
Jessy. St. John's Wood Road in those days
was quite in the country; on the other side of
the way, to the east where now is Lord's
Cricket Ground, was a sort of dairy-farm with
barns, haystacks, and pigstyes; in this place
Landseer made many studies of cows, horses,
pigs, &c.

Landseer, after living in the cottage for
some time, at last pulled it down and built the
house which was the one I remember. It
was small but rather aristocratic and dignified
in aspect; it had two large rooms which
served for studios, a billiard-room, a drawing-
room, and a tiny dining-room, this last small
room was lit by a skylight and the walls were
decorated with masterly sketches in charcoal
by Sir Edwin's own hand.

Landseer used only one of the large studios,
the other being generally filled with lumber;

the one he painted in was lit by a large
ordinary window, with the lower part covered
up : it was a gloomy looking place, the light
just focussed on the easel at which he worked,
whilst darkness brooded over the rest of the
room, in which were other easels with canvases
on them that were abandoned for the time.
There was not the slightest attempt at
decoration or adornment anywhere about the
place. He had holland cloths fixed to the
top edge of all his canvases, which he pulled
down over his work the moment he left it.
He moved his largest pictures about his room
by himself, and resented any offers of assist-
ance.   In an armchair near a gloomy-looking
stove his collie bitch " Lass " generally lay
curled up.

Landseer was painfully nervous about
showing his work to any one ; sometimes he
would only allow you to see it as reflected in
the large glass. It was dangerous to make
any remark, even though it might be in
praise, as I once found out to my great

regret.   I had expressed my admiration for a
beautifully painted group of dead ptarmigan,
hares, &c., in a picture of his which also con-
tained many people's portraits ; the next
morning I was extremely astonished and
mortified at finding the whole group rubbed
out, some rocks and heather being substituted
in its place.   I asked him why he had done
this, as the group had appeared to me so
exquisitely painted ; he replied, " Yes, that's
just it, I am not going to have the fellows
say how much better I can paint fur and
feathers than flesh."

The picture on which this destruction
took place was that large one of the Queen
and the Prince Consort with the Prince
of Wales, Lady Jocelyn, and a number
of Highland attendants, which no doubt
you remember was exhibited in the exhibition of the Royal Academy in 1870.
It had been exhibited once before in a somewhat unfinished state in 1854.   I remember
quite well that it looked a much finer picture

As you kindly consented
to lend me your aid for
an hour I hope you can afford
to make good your intention
one hour — I am so
jaded by Mr Commands
& Mr Suggestions ~~that~~
that I am indeed as
Crazy as my three ad
the Boat Picture are ↯

any one hour before
~~three~~ Monday afternoon
is enough for me —
— I hope this may find
you still a neighbour"

Ever
Sincerely Yours

Landseer.

then in every respect than it did on its second
appearance.   I feel sure that the trouble that
Landseer had over this picture did more than
anything else to hasten his death.   It had
been in his studio for so many years that
some of the personages portrayed in it were
dead and the others of course greatly altered ;
he had worked on the faces from time to time,
often without nature, and had made so many
alterations that the surface was utterly ruined,
the freshly added colour sinking in and
becoming opaque and heavy a few days after
it was put on.   He used to scrape out with
bits of glass, which were broken to a curved
scimitar shape, and the floor in front of this
picture was frequently covered with paint
scrapings.

This picture was not sent to the Academy
until the day before the Private View ; it
arrived quite early in the morning, when the
servants were cleaning the rooms.   Sir Edwin
asked me to accompany him, to see his work
in its place, and we drove to the Academy

together.   After looking nervously at his
picture for a few moments he took my arm
and went round the other rooms of the exhibition ; I was struck by the kindly interest he
took on this occasion in the works of others,
particularly those by younger men, praising
them sincerely and freely, and making inquiries
of me as to the personalities of the painters ;
this evinced much large-heartedness on his part
when one knew how bitterly disappointed and
distressed he must have felt about his own
picture all the time.

To pass to more cheerful recollections, in
his garden at one time I remember a hind
was tethered, at another a ewe came to stay
with Sir Edwin about which he related an
interesting occurrence, imitating his man
William's voice.   A knock came to Landseer's bedroom door one morning before he
was out of bed, " Please Sir Hedwin, the old
sheep 'as 'ad a little lamb."   " Very well, I'll
be down directly ; " presently another knock,
" Please Sir Hedwin, the old sheep 'as 'ad

another little lamb," which was the fact, and
these St. John's Wood born lambs afterwards
became the models for the picture entitled
Twins.

Landseer had another story of how his
man came, one morning, to him with " Please,
Sir Hedwin, did you horder a lion?" The
fact being that one that had died at the Zoo
had been sent in a four-wheeled cab to
Landseer to paint from.

Sir Edwin said that when he travelled he
never troubled about his luggage, as William
was always most anxious as to its safety,
getting out at all big stations and junctions,
and making inquiries of the guard about it.
" How about them luggage?" " Well, what's
it like?" says the guard. " Why it's as black
as hink with a Hell on it."

Landseer had a good ear, was a first-rate
mimic, and could imitate almost any voice
either of man or brute. He was a true
friend to all animals; it was, I believe,
chiefly owing to his suggestion that limbs

of trees were placed in the dens of the
larger carnivora at the Zoo, and I well
remember how eagerly he took up the cause
of the dogs against their cruel mutilators in
the matter of ears, writing to the papers
some very characteristic letters. To one
advocate of the practice, who in a letter to
the *Field* had stated that clipping the ears
of dogs gave them in his opinion a clever
look, Landseer replied that if this writer
really thought so, he had better have his
own ears clipped as no doubt it would make
him look very clever. He abhorred bear-
ing reins and all such abominations. I
remember him once, at Hengler's Circus,
going on bitterly at the manner the horses'
heads were reined in, and testifying his
delight when in one scene a pony had its
head given it free from all reins.

This is scarcely one of my usual D.B.
letters, but the sight of the old place recalled
so many memories that I could not resist
recording them in one of these letters to you.

LETTER XXVI

14th August, 1895.

DEAR MARCO—Hardly any flowers, that I know, equal the evening primrose in its exquisite purity : a charm which is, no doubt, owing to the fact that their blooms are so suddenly expanded and of so short duration. To enjoy their spotless purity in perfection you must rise very early in the morning ; it is generally too dark when they first open, in the evening, to see them properly, and they go off very soon after midday. These flowers must expand very rapidly; one might almost imagine that if you were to sit and watch, a distinct motion would be apparent. In the morning the bud is but a tight roll, about an inch and a half or two inches long; late in the afternoon it is a lovely funnel-shaped cup often three inches across.

The colour has a luminous quality that no pigment we possess can at all approximate; generally of a delicate pure yellow, but sometimes white. *Œ. tarraxifolia* has very large white blooms, which are quite startling when you come upon them unexpectedly in the evening; the foliage greatly resembles that of the dandelion, hence its name, but the habit of the plant is straggling and untidy, which, together with the fact that the blooms change to a rather dull pink as they go off, somewhat detracts from the value of the plant in my eyes. *Œnothera missouriensis* has yellow flowers nearly as large as *Œ. tarraxifolia*, the foliage being compact and of a lovely sub-

dued green with stems of a coral colour ; it
is a very satisfactory plant, and when grown
on the edge of a wall, coming up through a
carpeting of stone-crop, as mine is, nothing
can exceed its beauty. The flowers of *Œ.
mis.* as they go off change to a rich orange
colour, which in no way injures the general
effect in the daytime. I care not for the
tall biennial *Œnothera biennis*, as the fading
blooms on this are too much in evidence,
suggesting a slatternly woman in curl-papers.
The little perennial, *Œ. fructicosa*, commonly known as "sun-drops," is a capital
plant for the border ; its blossoms last well
through the day and are produced in great
abundance ; but it must have either a wet
season or plenty of watering to keep it
thriving in perfection, as if it gets dry it
droops and looks miserable directly. It
blooms earlier in the year than most of its
family do, in May and June with me.
Then there is a delightful annual sort,
Œ. odorata, sweet-scented as its name

implies. I sowed some patches of this rather more, I think, than eight years ago, and though I have sown none since, I have never been without numbers of self-sown plants, coming up amidst the general tangle in the autumn, which are ever welcome, not alone for their lively beauty and profusion of bloom, but for their sweet scent, which is of a purity and innocence in harmony with their aspect, and which greatly resembles that of the cowslip. It is most refreshing, as the autumn comes on, to be thus reminded that there is such a period as spring. Most of the evening primroses seed very freely, some night-feeding insect no doubt doing the necessary fertilisation. The corolla of *Œ. tarraxifolia* is joined to the ovary by quite five inches of slender tube; the stamens are situated round the entrance of this tube, the pistil going down its entire length; on page 75 of my former Letters is a drawing of its curiously-shaped seed-pod.

[*To face page* 206.

ŒNOTHERA MISSOURIENSIS,

There are numbers of flowers, like the
evening primroses, that can only be seen in
their true glory as they grow.   The blossom
of the beautiful mock orange or syringa
(*Philodelphum grandiflora*) is never satisfactory when gathered, but a bush in full
bloom as seen against a blue sky affords one
of the most lovely visions that any garden
can produce ; to my mind it surpasses both
cherry and apple-blossom ; there is a creamy
character about the white flowers which
renders them more harmonious against the
blue than the pure white of the cherry, and I
prefer their serene beauty to the gaiety of the
apple-blossom.

The bushes throw up overhead strong
arching shoots, often six or eight feet long,
thickly laden with scented flower clusters,
each in individual detail equalling in beauty
the orange blossom of the bridal bouquet.
Beyond this one glorious display the shrub
has little to boast of in the way of interest.

As far as I can see it has no berries or

seed-pods, its foliage is in no way remarkable, and the long arching shoots, devoid of
bloom, present a straggling and untidy
appearance. It is no evergreen, and is seldom selected as a nesting place by birds, but
it is thoroughly hardy, needs no care, and
never fails in its one glorious display, unless
when grown in a smoky atmosphere, being
essentially a country subject.

Although I am really fond of plants and
flowers I am a wretched hand at arranging
them prettily when cut. I believe I am too
anxious about it, as sometimes, quite by
accident, when I throw the flowers together
without any definite idea or plan pretty combinations occur. Some people have a gift in
this matter. Most ladies *think* they can do
it well, but really very few excel in the art.
The flower arrangements at dinner tables are
seldom in perfect taste; there is great lack of
originality as well, any pretty idea as to com-
bination being imitated *ad nauseam*. To my
mind flowers on a table are seldom treated

as reverently as they deserve to be ; as a rule
people are far too lavish in the use they
make of flowers for decorative purposes. A
few set off and telling at their best are
worth hundreds squandered by vulgar
opulence.

After all, flowers look far best when seen
growing, especially if they are allowed to
have their own way, sow themselves, and
struggle amongst one another in sweet confusion ; the beauty of the more brilliant being
greatly enhanced by the neutral tints of their
surroundings, towards which setting-off even
decay assists, as well as do numberless plants
of sober tints and bizarre character ; such,
for instance as *Gypsophila paniculata*, sea
lavender, plume poppy, sea holly, mullein,
rosemary, lavender, sedums, saxifrages and
the like.

My niece, Katie, has a great natural gift
for flower arrangement, she has placed, to-
day, a beaker filled with a huge bunch of
gypsophila, amongst which are a dozen of

the steely blue heads of the globe thistle ; as seen against a background of Dutch tiles the effect of this is extremely captivating.   She wanders about my garden in the morning, in a quiet sort of way, picking up here and there little unconsidered trifles, with which she manages afterwards to produce charming and novel combinations.   It is wonderful what she can do with the fading foliage of the pœony in late autumn.   In fact I am continually being delighted and surprised by her graceful ingenuity.

LETTER XXVII

Neighbour's Rookery Deserted—Reasons for—Kingfisher—Its
Flight—Hovering—Kingfisher in India—Kingfisher's and Humming Bird Moth's Wings Compared—Wych Elms—Gainsborough's Tree—Sudbury—The Seaside.

24th August, 1895.

DEAR MARCO—My neighbour's rookery
this year has been entirely deserted. In the
spring some nests were begun as usual, but
a severe gale in April carried away one or
two, and shortly afterwards the rest were
abandoned by the old birds. He tells me
that there has been a marked decrease in the
number of nests each year lately ; and now
the trees are completely forsaken. One or
two reasons are suggested for this desertion,
first, the old and oft-repeated opinion, that it
is because the practice of shooting the young

P 2

rooks had been given up for several years. Next, that the great flood last year, and the severity and frequency of the gales of wind in the springs of recent years, had alarmed the rooks as to the safety of the trees, which are very near the edge of the river; and a third reason was, that possibly it was owing to the fact of several pairs of brown owls having taken up their abode in the trees close to the rookery. As to these owls, I believe that they came across the river to build in my neighbour's garden in the spring of last year, frightened out of their usual nesting places in some elms by the hammering and noise of the preparations for the Agricultural Show, just as were the wood-pigeons mentioned in a former letter.

I can hardly suppose, however, that the rooks would have cared a bit for the owls, though possibly they may have objected to having their night's rest disturbed by their hooting.

I see "our" kingfisher now frequently.

The flight of this bird is, I am quite sure,
more remarkable for its absolute straightness
than for its swiftness. The evenness and well-
sustained rapidity of the beat of its wings, set
far back on the awkwardly shaped body, is
the chief characteristic of the bird's flight : it
never closes its wings to make a swoop, or
flies in undulating curves, as swallows and
many other birds do.

As to the occasional hovering of the kingfisher alluded to in Letter XIII. of my former
series, a friend, Colonel Luard, writes to me :
" In India the gray kingfisher, which is the
one most frequently seen, invariably hovers
so far as I know, but I should have said with
his beak almost vertically downwards. The
fluttering of the wings is extremely rapid."

The position of the wings on the kingfisher is very much like that of the wings on
a humming-bird moth, and as this hovers
continually in its flight, it seems reasonable
to suppose that the bird could also hover
easily.

I have several wych elms in my garden,
three of them on the edge of the river,
over which their branches hang and bend
down in the most graceful manner. The
foliage and habit of this tree is excessively
beautiful, a great contrast to that of the
ordinary hedge-row elm, which has been
characterised by Professor Ruskin as " sticking
its elbows out in an awkward fashion." The
leaves are longer and more pointed than those
of the common elm, and the branches have a
tendency to weep. This is the tree which
Gainsborough so frequently introduces into
his backgrounds, and which he renders by a
flimsy conventional sort of execution which
is familiar to all lovers of his works. At
times his rendering of the tree is objectionable
from its extreme carelessness, but it is never
without a distinct indication of the character
of the tree intended to be represented.

Until I had been to Sudbury, his birthplace,
in Suffolk, I never gave Gainsborough credit
for much attempt at truth to nature in the

treatment of his foliage.   But in the beautifully wooded and undulating parks and
meadows, which abound in that vicinity, the
prevailing tree is the wych elm, and I was
reminded of his lovely landscapes and back-
grounds on every side.   If a man has any
soul at all the trees he knew best as a boy
remain his favourites to the end of his life.

We leave here next week for a change of
air at the seaside.   Much I grudge it, as I
cannot bear to be away from my garden for
any length of time.   Boscombe, near Bournemouth, is our destination, but one seaside place
is as bad as another to me now ; after the
first three days' pleasure in inhaling the ozone,
the monotony and seasidedness of the thing
palls on me dreadfully.

LETTER XXVIII

12th September, 1895.

DEAR MARCO—Many happy returns of the day (to-morrow)* to you. We are still at the seaside, but return, probably, next week to Wallingford. I have enjoyed this place more than I anticipated, chiefly owing to the wonderfully warm and summerlike weather that has continued ever since we have been here. By far the best thing in this neighbourhood is the Abbey Church at Christchurch, which reminds me much of St. Albans before

* The 13th of September, Mr. Marks's birthday.

it was spoilt.   The carving in the choir,
the Norman work in the nave and the north-
west porchway, which is early decorated, are
all very well worth seeing.   I made a couple
of little outline sketches, one of the little
canopied quatrefoil in the porch and another
from the northern end of the transept, which
I enclose, though I dare say you know the
place well.   Whilst drawing in the porchway
I was much struck by the contrast of some
restored mouldings to the older work; the
old work had the look of being all alive and
growing, whilst the other seemed as dead as
the stone it was carved in.   I could not convey this living look to the lines of my sketch
try all I knew, though I think I could have
given something of it if I had taken a week
over it with colour and brushes.

The coast scenery in this neighbourhood
must have been wonderfully fine before the
public found out Bournemouth; sandy gorse-
clad cliffs and chines of the most picturesque
character, as good as Hampstead Heath in the

North Transept, Christchurch.

days of our youth, backed up by pine-woods
with undergrowth of bracken and brambles.

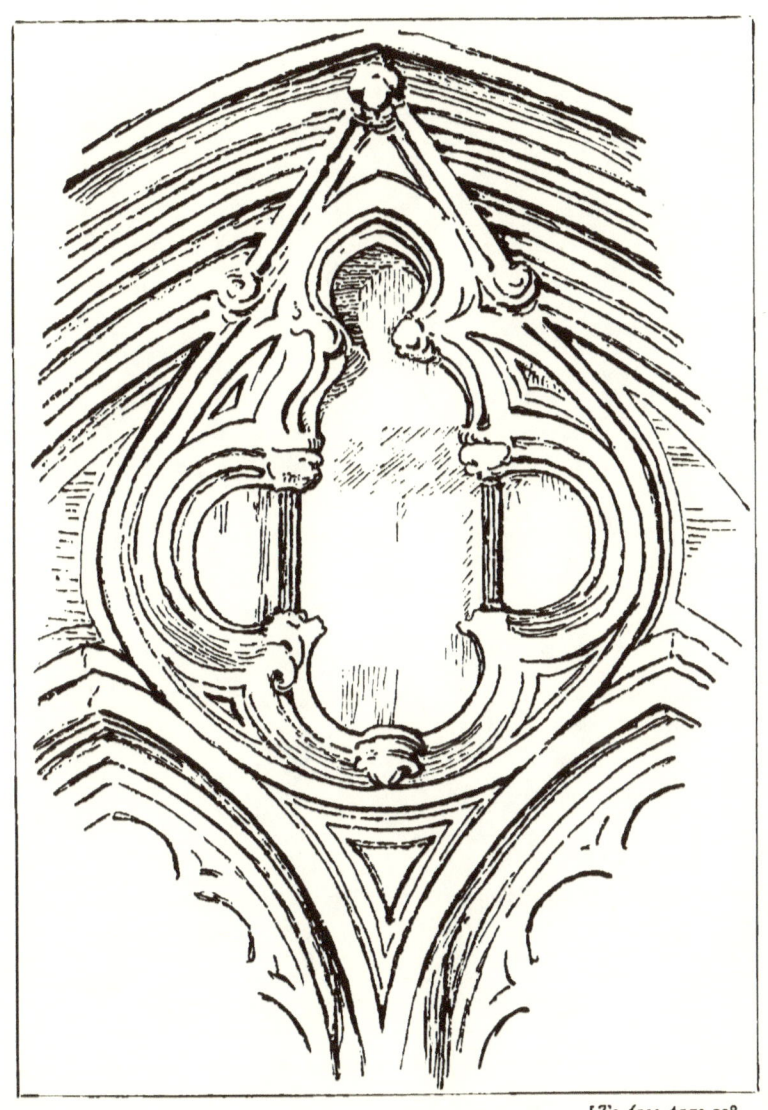

[To face page 218.

FROM THE NORTH PORCH, CHRISTCHURCH.

One or two patches, here and there, still remain, but the rest has been badly raddled by villas, huge hotels, lodging-houses, rows of shops, roads, lamp-posts and corporation gardens— buildings of one sort and another extending along the coast for more than seven miles of what must have been its prettiest part. Every villa, large or small, rejoices in some fine-sounding name, and has from one to a great number of the indigenous pine-trees still standing in its garden or grounds. To me it seems very sad, but I suppose it cannot be helped. The beach and bathing are splendid, however, and my children, who I am glad to say are all strong swimmers, enjoyed themselves immensely.

In my last letter I wrote about the wych elm as essentially Gainsborough's tree, some fine young sweet chestnuts that I noticed in this neighbourhood reminded me that this may truly be considered Titian's tree, for it is the one he most frequently introduces in his backgrounds. These trees, I am told, flourish

abundantly in the vicinity of his birthplace,
and thus, as in Gainsborough's case, the tree
familiar to Titian as a boy became the
favourite one throughout his long life.   He
is especially fond of representing this tree in
its picturesque old age as a gnarled stump
from which shoot out a lusty young growth of
branch and foliage ; a habit of rejuvenescence
which is one of the great charms of the sweet
chestnut.   Titian loved the tree, as well for
its grand and laurel-like foliage, its massive
yet graceful form, the lustre and richness of
the colour of its leaves, and the swing and
curves of its branches.   Here, in England,
we ought to have many more of these trees
than we do, in our parks and plantations.
They are abundant in parts of Kent.   I recollect some very fine ones in a park near
Brenchley, and numbers are grown as sap-
lings in the coppices and woods in the vicinity
of the hop-districts, for these chestnuts make
the best of hop-poles, lasting longer, I was
told, than those made from hazel or any other

tree. The foliage, especially when the fruit
begins to show, is beautiful from any point of
view, but as seen against a deep blue sky,
with a white cloud or two on it, the effect is
perfectly glorious; both Titian and Paul
Veronese often so introduced it into their
pictures. The foliage of this tree will not
stand any scamping or sketchy treatment, it
demands great mastery of drawing and
vigorous colouring, or the effect of its gran-
deur is lost. One seldom sees it represented
in the works of the modern impressionist
school of landscape painters, who prefer trees
such as the willow or poplar, that can be
fairly well suggested by smudges of tone with
dabs of light behind them. The Spanish
chestnut cannot be *suggested*, it can only be
rendered in its massive dignity by the patience
of true genius.

I noticed one day last week a number of
sand-martins hawking over the sea, some
distance from the shore, just as they do over
our river. I was puzzled to know what they

could be after ; I went out in a boat afterwards with my boys, and we noticed a number of little winged ants flying over the waves,
some fallen into the water too.   The wind
was from off the shore and it was a very hot
day, and no doubt there must have been some
ant-swarming going on amongst the sandy
pine-woods from which these winged ants
had got carried out to sea.   The sand-martins
every now and then took dips in the water ; I
at first thought that they did this to clean
themselves from vermin, preparatory to their
long flight, but I am convinced now that they
were really after the little flies which they
snapped up from the surface at times.

THE ISLE OF WIGHT, FROM BOSCOMBE.

[*To face page* 222.

LETTER XXIX

14th October, 1895.

DEAR MARCO—Many letters have appeared in the papers giving accounts of the vagaries of plant life which have taken place in consequence of the extraordinary warmth which prevailed during the last month. I noticed some such phenomenal events in our garden, as, for instance, an apple-tree with ripe fruit and fresh blossom on it, a second crop of raspberries, and a laburnum with patches of blossom and young leaves here and there, whilst the seed-pods were still hanging on it.

This lovely autumn recalls to my mind the fortnight in October that you and I spent at Wargrave years ago. I remember the number of glow-worms that we saw then ; they are just as plentiful in this neighbourhood at present. My daughter brought one home yesterday, as well as one of those luminous centipedes about which I wrote in Letter VIII. (former series). I put both these creatures into the garden, they seemed very lively and well, but I hardly think that we shall see them any more, judging from the failure of former similar experiments.

My wife and I paid a short visit last week to some friends residing at Langford, a small village in the south-west corner of Oxfordshire, not very far from W. Morris's house at Kelmscot. The church at Langford is an extremely interesting one, parts of the structure being possibly of Saxon work, or at any rate very early Norman. Its chief curiosity is a " vested " crucifix, which is on the outside of the east wall of the porch. The figure is sunken in a sort of panel, the bounding stones of which are evidently as old as the figure itself, for several of them are of that pinky-coloured stone so commonly seen in the old

Vested Crucifix at Langford Church.

Norman churches of Oxfordshire and Berkshire. The figure is life-size, the head missing, the body clothed in a long tunic with a girdle round the loins. The arms are perfectly horizontal, the feet separate and straight, and there are no nails or wounds in

Q

either the hands or feet. I do not think
that this figure has always been in the place
where it is now, most probably it was originally on an inner wall of the church itself; the
present porch appears to be of comparatively
modern date, perhaps built in the time of
Queen Elizabeth when the church was restored; the crucifix itself was in all likelihood
carved in the seventh century. This vested
crucifix is unique in our islands; there are
several in France and Italy, and a few in
Germany. No crucifix *at all* is known earlier
than the sixth century, and up to the end of
the seventh century the figure was always
entirely clothed, as this one is. Sometimes a
crown (not of thorns) is seen on the head, and
rich embroidery on the vestment. After the
seventh century the vestment was shortened,
and in time a sort of kilt remained as the only
clothing. The realistic treatment of the
crucifix is, comparatively, quite a modern
idea, the figure never having been represented as hanging from the nailed hands, or
crowned with thorns, until the thirteenth cen-

tury.   Up to that time the arms were horizontal, the feet separate, and the loins amply
clothed.

On the front of the porch, over the
entrance, is another crucifix, also em-
panelled, of a later period than the other.
It bears unmistakable evidence of having
been removed at some time, as the arms of
our Lord and the figures of St. John and
the Virgin have been reversed, the left hand
stones having taken the place of those on
the right, and *vice versâ*, which gives the
arms a very ugly appearance, whilst the
figures below look away from the cross
instead of towards it.   Over this porch, or
a much older one, there has been a
parvise or priest's room, the entrance to
which, with the steps of ascent, are still
plainly visible on the wall inside the church.
On the tower, which is very old and
massive, there are the remains of a sun-
dial with two little figures supporting it ;
these figures look to me very like some of
those in the Bayeux tapestry.

I went, on my friend's tricycle, to see
another old church not very far off, which,
though cruelly restored, has a lovely stone
spire and a decorated Norman porch of
highly elaborated design. It was old
Michaelmas Day, and all the country people
were, as is the custom, on the move. They
call this day here "Flitting Day." I remember that in Denmark there is also such
a day, which is called "Flit Dag." I met
in every direction those large picturesque
farm wains, which are yellow and red in
colour, and beautiful in line and curve; the
farmers goodnaturedly lend these to the
moving cottagers, who pile them up with
their household goods; one such wain, with
sometimes a two-wheeled cart, holding the
whole family possessions comfortably. The
goods were of a curiously mixed description:
chests of drawers, fire-irons, bundles of bed-
ding, faggots, tubs of cabbage plants and
flowers; generally a magpie or a blackbird
in a cage, with women and children on the
top of all. The entire day is given up to

this flitting business, little or no work going
on in the fields ; the cottagers who are not
themselves moving, stand about gossiping at
their garden gates and chaffing the passing
flitters.   I am told that old Michaelmas Day
is " Flit Day " for agricultural cottagers all
over England, but I have never noticed the
occurrence myself before.

It has been a wonderful season for apples
and pears ; ours have been very fine and
plentiful.   I am not sure but that I admire
an apple-tree in fruit almost as much as one
in blossom, there is a solidity in the glory of
the fruit which is very satisfactory ; and the
contrast it affords when seen against a deep
blue sky is even more beautiful than that of
the blossom.   More beautiful still than even
the apple-tree when seen thus, is a quince-
tree with its handsome foliage and magnificent golden fruit ; such a one grows in the
Rev. C. Wodehouse's garden at Langford,
on the lawn ; I can give you no idea how
splendid it looked in the autumn sunshine.
The colour of the fruit is a delicious mixture

of gold and lemon, overladen here and there with the dusky grey *down* which is so characteristic of the quince, and which gives it its Latin and Italian names of *Malus Cotonea* and *Mele cotogne* (Gerard).

What good jelly and marmalade quinces make ! Alice has this year made a quantity from the quinces off my own tree, which is only a small one at present, but when its roots get down to the level of the brook by which it is planted it will grow rapidly. The smell of quinces, when gathered, is rather overpowering in a room, but on a sunny day the scent from a tree with ripe fruit on it is most delicious as you pass it by. By the way, true *marmalade* is made of quinces, what we generally know as such ought to be called "*orange* marmalade"; I found this out from Gerard, who gives the Spanish names for the quince, *Membrilhos* and *Marmellos*. He gives also the following good recipe : "Take faire Quinces, pare them, cut them in peeces, and cast away the core, then put unto every pound of Quinces a

pound of Sugar, and to every pound of sugar
a pint of water: these must be boiled
togither over a still fire untill they be very
soft, then let it be strained or rather rubbed
through a strainer, or an hairie sieve which
is better, and then set it over the fire to
boile againe, untill it be stiffe, and so boxe it
up, and as it cooleth put thereto a little rose
water, and a few grains of muske, well
mingled together, which will give a goodly
taste unto the Cotiniat.   This is the way to
make Marmalade."

A few martins still hawk over the river,
and the starlings and robins make the
garden cheerful, the first with the wonderful
"variety entertainment" which they give
every morning, and the second with their
sweet little autumnal songs.   I never recollect seeing such numbers of gnats as
during the last fortnight, but, I am happy to
say, they do not come into the house very
much.

LETTER XXX

26th November, 1895.

DEAR MARCO—The wind has nipped everything in my garden, so that it is absolutely
flowerless now.   The previous cold snap, on
the 26th and 27th of last month, had, however,
already finished off most things ; my favourite
China roses suffered especially, in spite of the
mild weather that followed.   I have not picked
a bud from them since ; often in other years
I have gathered lovely bunches in December.
My wild chrysanthemums in the glasshouse
come in very usefully this year, they are

wonderfully full of bloom ; I have gathered
again and again, literally, armfuls, and still
quantities remain : these and the pyracantha
berries are nearly the only things we have for
indoor decoration.

There is very little work for me in the
flower borders at present, except tidying up
and weeding, and even that is now stopped
by the bitter wind, it is so strong that it even
prevents me from enjoying the delicious perfume of the bonfires, which at this season are
continually burning, but which require a calm,
still, misty day for their true appreciation.
As to weeds, I have come to the conclusion
that the only way to keep the borders free
from them is to allow no space for them to
grow in ; to have every inch of the ground
covered with cultivated plants ; no bare
spaces of mould showing anywhere, at any
rate during the spring and summer. It is
astonishing how soon nature clothes with
vegetation all bare places even in the most
unlikely spots. In that beautiful water-colour

drawing which I have, by G. P. Boyce, (a view of Farringdon Street and Smithfield, taken at the time when enormous blocks of houses were removed to make room for the underground railway), there is a great heap of sandy earth and rubbish in the foreground over which delicate young grass and weeds have already spread themselves. It was, I am convinced, the sight of this effort of nature to reassert herself, as much as anything else, that caused the artist to select this curious scene for his subject. These poor little weeds could only have had one season in which to establish themselves and make the best of it amidst the ruins. When we consider the miles of houses and chimney-pots with which the place was surrounded, it is difficult to imagine how the seeds could have so quickly reached it.

Grass is a strange and perverse thing, growing only too freely where it is little wanted or expected, whilst it frequently perishes on lawns and places in which it is desired. It is one of the worst of all the weeds that trouble my flower borders, persistently getting into the clumps of crocuses and carpeting plants, from whence it is extremely difficult of extraction without disturbing the whole spot. In weeding I collect all the grass with its roots in a basket by itself, and use it to patch bare places on the lawn, but I am sorry to say with only partial success. In seasons of drought my lawns, owing to the porous subsoil, look very shabby, and I am much humiliated on coming to town to see the grass that grows on the roof of the smoking-room at the Athenæum Club, looking far healthier and greener than any that I have here. Perhaps the warmth of the room below has something to do with it, or possibly the artificial watering which it receives from the hose may be the secret, at any rate I have seldom seen healthier-looking grass.

Of all grasses the twitch, or couch, as a weed is the worst ; next to this is the fine-leaved creeping or running grass, of which I have a great abundance. I have drawn out, at times, lengths of six or seven feet of this grass from yew hedges and shrubs, amongst which it had grown up ; it does not seem to mind meeting with no earth in which to root itself during its upward growth, but stretches up and up towards the light. Sometimes, as in the case of some lavender bushes I have, it spreads itself so thickly amongst the branches as to nearly choke the shrub.

About a fortnight ago we saw a solitary gull, a small one with a white head (I will not venture on a name this time) hawking over the river, near Mougewell. We watched it flying up and down for some time, until suddenly a carrion crow flew after it, seeming bent on either killing it or driving it away. It attacked the gull persistently, and though the latter flew swiftly and easily, apparently taking little heed of its enemy, I was anxious about it ; the crow seemed to fly quite as quickly, and made repeated dabs at it with its beak, so, when they were both rather near me, I waved my stick and shouted as loud as I could, which alarmed the crow and he made off, and soon afterwards the gull went in another direction.

Carrion crows are not very common about here, they can easily be mistaken for rooks; they are, however, a trifle smaller, and if anything more glossy, and have not the whitish excrescence over their beaks which characterises the rook; they are generally seen in pairs and haunt some particular locality. The one in question was one of a pair that had their nest in a horse-chestnut tree close by the spot where the attack on the gull took place; I have noticed this pair repeatedly at that part of the river, usually seeing them feeding on the banks, I should say on dead fish or mussels.

In shape the bird greatly resembles a raven, and its note is more like a raven's croak than a rook's caw. I am told that they are very fierce birds, and that they often attack other birds, sometimes pecking out their eyes, and that they are reported to do the same to rabbits and even sheep.

In weeding the other day I came upon a thing of great beauty, namely,—a berry of the lily-of-the-valley; this well-known favourite seldom seeds, though in the spring its flowers are much beset by bees; I have been told that it is seldom known to have more than one berry on a stem. The berry I found was the only one in quite a large patch of faded plants, but it was most lovely, I really think for exquisite colouring more beautiful than any berry I ever saw. Chinese vermilion, I should say, approximates nearest to its tint; it had a delicate bloom on its surface, was large and elegant in shape, and gained very much by the contrast of its pure colour with the neutral tints which surrounded it. There it hung complete and spotless amidst the *débris* of decaying leaves. You will, I dare say, laugh at me for my sentimentality, but I cannot tell you what inexpressible pleasure a thing of this sort gives me.

LETTER XXXI

January 20th, 1896.

DEAR MARCO—The following extracts, which I have selected from some of the many letters that came to me after the publication of my former volume, are far too interesting to be consigned to the limbo of an appendix, so I incorporate them in a final etter to you. They mostly take the shape

of emendation and correction, and I gladly
avail myself of the opportunity, which the
kindness and courtesy of these correspondents
has afforded me, of setting right certain
blunders which I made through ignorance.

Alluding to some rather disparaging
remarks of mine as to the character of the
song of the blackbird Sir George Grove
writes thus :—

"Are you quite right in what you say
about the blackbird? He is a very old
friend of mine, and unless I have been wrong
for thirty years it is the thrush and not he
that is to blame for the 'reiteration in his
song.' The thrush gets
a short phrase, such as
of two or three notes,
and then gives it over and over again six
or seven times—very brilliantly, but merely
over and over ; whereas the blackbird is quite
different, he selects a spot where he is
within hearing of a comrade ; and then he
begins quite at leisure (not all in a hurry like

the thrush) a regular conversation—'And how are you? Isn't this a fine day? Let us have a nice talk,' &c. &c. He is answered in the same strain, and then replies, and so on. Nothing more thoughtful, more refined, more feeling, can be conceived. Iteration is the last thing to be objected to in his song.

"Am I wrong (I think I can't be), or have you mistaken the thrush for the blackbird? Pardon me for all this, but tell me if I am right or wrong."

Sir George is quite right, and when I answered his kind letter I owned up my error manfully. His letter continues :—

"As to his 'chuck-chuck-chuck,' that, I suppose, is what gave us Tennyson's lines in the 'Early Spring,'

> 'Till at thy chuckled note,
> Thou twinkling bird,'

by which that great observer of nature has well expressed not only the alarm-call but the swift way in which the bird flits past while he calls."

R

In another letter Sir George writes :—

" I love the robins in autumn as much as you do. To me they always say ' Why is the summer gone and the cold weather coming on ? ' I love them, but they fill a much smaller part than the blackbird does in my heart. To hear the blackbird talking to his mate a field off, with deliberate, refined conversation, the very acme of grace and courtesy, is perfectly splendid. The thrush is more intense, but he falls below the other."

I have received many letters in which an error I made as to the blossoming of the tulip tree is alluded to and corrected. I had thought that these trees only bloomed in our country in very hot seasons, the real fact being that, after the tree has attained a good age, it blooms every year. I select the correction of this error that came in a letter from my friend F. Smallfield, R.W.S., as it is perhaps the most explicit and interesting.

" The footnote, p. 202, tempts me to a bit of reminiscence. In my native village,

which I did not finally quit until I was twelve
years old, there grew a splendid tulip tree;
for eight of these twelve years I was
capable of noticing the tree (my father was a
great tree-planter, and taught us to look at
flowering trees) and it blossomed every year
most luxuriantly. The tree was a mass of
orange and green lyre-shaped cups between
June and July. This tree flourished much
nearer London than your remembered tree
in Cashiobury Park. There is a superb
specimen in the garden of Taplow House,
Taplow ; it is stated to be the oldest specimen
in England ; but that kind of reputation is
much like the fable as to the rarity of the
Judas tree, or centenarianism in the human
being. In the garden at Taplow House
there is a Judas tree, as one also at Salt Hill,
Slough, in a garden opposite the Windmill
Inn. Doubtless there are scores more to be
seen, if we look and inquire, of Judas trees,
as of the Catalpa, another lovely flowering
tree, which you must have noticed in the

garden at Dulwich College when going there
to choose works for the R.A. students, or
for the 'Old Masters' shows.' My father
planted a Catalpa which was one of the
summer glories of our garden. Taplow
House, now inhabited by Mr. Walter Barron
and his family, was formerly the residence of
the Marquis of Thomond; I can fancy Sir
Joshua's niece plucking armfuls of tulip tree
blossoms, as I have seen the little Barron
girls, from the branches that sweep the lawn.
Theophila Palmer in a white gown, and laden
with branches of tulip tree in flower, would
have made a good portrait-model for her
uncle.

"It is curious how we live with certain
plants almost under our eyes and do not
notice them. *You* say you never but once
before had seen the tulip tree blossom; until
last summer *I* had never seen the water
violet. My daughter and self walking in a
lane near the 'Welsh Harp' came upon a
pond filled with the plant—which we at

first mistook for the bog-bean—a mass of flowers. I carried some to a lady botanical professor, in order to obtain the name. There is a purple-flowered variety of the tulip tree I am told."

Mr. Smallfield also sets me right as to the proper derivation of the name " Dwale " for the deadly nightshade, sending me the following extract from Halliwell's *Dictionary of Archaic and Provincial Words :—*

" Dwale. The nightshade (Anglo-Saxon). It is highly narcotic, and hence used to express a lethargic disease. See *Relig. Antiq.*, i. 324, for a curious receipt in which it is mentioned. There was a sleeping potion so called, made of hemlock and other materials, which is alluded to by Chaucer, and was given formerly to patients on whom surgical operations were to be performed.

" *To dwale*, to mutter deliriously ; a Devonshire verb, which seems to be connected with other times.

When as Joseph had told this tale,
Thei fel as thei had drunken *dwale*,
Grovelynge doun on erthe flat.

Cursor Mundi.
M. S. Coll. Trin., Cantab.

For I wel knowe be thy tale,
That thou hast drunken of the *dwale*.

Gower.
M. S., Soc. Ant.

" The same book also gives *Dwain* as an adj., meaning 'faint, sickly'; and as a noun, meaning a 'swoon or fainting fit': and *Dwallowed* as meaning 'withered.'"

In Jameson's *Dictionary of the Scottish Language* the following words are found which also seem to have their origin from *Dwale*.

" Dualm, Dwalm, Dwaum, *s.*   I. A swoon.   2. A sudden fit of sickness.

" Dualmyng, Dwauming, *s.*   I. A swoon. 2. Metaph : The fall of the evening.

" To Dwaum, *v.a.*   To fade : to decline in health.   " It is still said in this sense, ' He dwaum'd away.'"   (Jameson's *Diction-*

ary of the Scottish Language.   Nimmo,
London and Edinburgh.   1885.)

Canon Ellacombe, writing from Bitton
Vicarage, sent me some extremely interesting
notes and corrections.   Referring to my remarks on "the velvet rose" he writes :—

"For many years I have collected and
grown the old roses—I am pleased to hear
that you have Gerard's velvet rose ; it, however, is surely wretchedly drawn by Gerard
—Parkinson's plate is a little better.   I have
grown it for many years, having found it in
a Devonshire garden.   It is known as the
Tuscany rose, and as that was described and
figured in the *Bot. Reg.* of 1820.   It is one
of the darkest roses I know and very
velvety."

This on the yellow crocus, p. 30, of *Letters
to Marco.*

"In confirmation of what you say, I have
been told that pale yellow is now considered
a better protection against sun than white—
the photographers have found that out for us."

On swallows, p. 35.

" It is not quite correct to say that swallows are allied to humming birds—swifts are and have been removed from the Hirundines in consequence."

On snails, p. 56.

" Snails, &c., eating decaying plants.   Is not that exactly what we do ? and hang our meat for the purpose ?   Ripe fruit is really fruit beginning to decay.   The Persians eat the peach *green*."

On the Crown Imperial, p. 74.

"—' Like a mace.'—It is so, but it gets its name from the top of the seed-vessel being the exact representation of the old Imperial Crown of the Eastern and other kings."

On leaves and raindrops, p. 78.

" I believe you will find almost a con-sensus of botanists that no leaf can imbibe moisture.   It gives out moisture, but gets all it wants *ab intra* and not *ab extra*—just like moist skin."

On the venom of toads, p. 93.

"The best authorities, such as Bell's
British Reptiles, deny the poisonous character of the toad's exudation ; it is acrid, and
that is all."

Canon Ellacombe further corrects me for
stating that "robins do not pack," for he
says that they do when they migrate.

I am sure all lovers of gardens must be,
as I am, grateful to Canon Ellacombe for
the delightful book he has just written on
his Gloucestershire garden.

Mr. R. Scot Skirving, Edinburgh, referring
to the statement of the farmer that rams
pastured in a meadow caused mushrooms to
grow in it, writes :

" Every book I have read on the artificial
growth of mushrooms contains some sentence
like this : ' Use horse-dung for manure,
strange to say that of entire horses is said
to be the best.' This is easily explained.
Entire horses are much more highly fed than
other horses, and therefore their dung is

richer. The same may be said of rams used for breeding, but I should think it would require the meadow to be *small* and the rams *numerous* to produce any effect."

Mr. Skirving also asks me a question about my plant *Dictamnus fraxinella.* This plant is supposed to emit from its blossom when fully out a certain gas which ignites on a flame being put to it; and I had said that I should anxiously look forward to the blooming period so as to try the experiment myself. I am sorry I cannot satisfy Mr. Skirving's curiosity, for my root of *D. frax.* was but a tiny scrap of a thing when I obtained it from the nurseryman; it was badly eaten by a slug the first year, since then it has grown very little and, in spite of the great care I have taken of it, has not yet bloomed. The plant is a proverbially slow grower; mine dies down to the very ground every year in the most alarming manner, but comes up again the following spring. It looks healthy, but is still quite small. I hope to live to see it

bloom and to try the experiment.*   I was led
to great expectations by the representation
given of the plant in the nurseryman's cata-
logue.   The illustrations in these catalogues
must always be regarded with extreme caution
or disappointment will frequently ensue : then
again, nurserymen have a way of sending you
such tiny specimens of the plants you order,
that unless great care is taken, they perish
soon after you have planted them.   The fine
clumps of good things that I have had given
me from time to time by generous friends
have never failed to prosper.

Mrs. Hawkins, of Ilfracombe, to whom I
am indebted for some bee stories given in
Letter XII., also sent me the following interesting notes on starlings and rooks :—

"You say the starling is infested with
vermin, so also is the house-martin to an
alarming degree.   The martin, unlike

* In a letter that I received quite recently, Mr. Skirving informs
me that he has since verified for himself, in the Botanical Gardens at
Edinburgh, the curious property that this plant possesses of emitting
inflammable gas.

the puffin, has no general spring cleaning.
The puffin gets several of her species to
assist in clearing out her nest, previous to
laying her one egg, while, as the house-
swallow generally has three successive broods
in a season, her one nest gets filled with
vermin. I should like to give you an
anecdote of the starling which came under
my own observation. In the winter of 1888,
while visiting in Wiltshire, there were about
300 of these saucy birds pecking about on
the snow-covered meadow, when suddenly
the son of my host shot into them, wound-
ing however only one, which struggled painfully alone on the snow, but not for long,
for back flew one of its mates to perch
beside it, and comfort it as best it could in
its own bird language.

"I used to like to watch the rooks in our
rookery in the building season. They
always leave a sentinel or two behind to
guard the half-formed nests in the home
trees, and occasionally the naughty sentinel

robs a stick from his neighbour's nest for
his own ; but the returning rook instantly
detects the theft and summons another to
assist in administering a good pecking as
punishment for the offence."

The Rev. Theodore Mayo, Quatford
House, Bridgnorth, in an obliging note in
which he refers to my mistake about the tulip
tree, adds : "About two months ago I went
to call at a house in this neighbourhood where
its present inhabitants have lived for thirteen
or fourteen years. The lady took me into
the garden and said : 'We are watching our
tulip tree with great interest to see the
flowers—you see it is in bud.' I answered,
'I am sorry to disappoint you, those are not
buds but seed-vessels.' I broke one and
showed her that it was a seed-vessel and
drew her attention to the peculiar aromatic
smell. I believe the flowers are frequently
overlooked, as they have been in this case.
They are not conspicuous, and look very
much like leaves prematurely dead.

"With regard to that curious light in animals' eyes I have seen it more often in dogs' eyes than in cats'. I think I may say that I have seen it in the case of each companion dog that I have had during my life. I have also seen it in certain human eyes. I mean in the eyes of certain individuals, but I think in those of children only. It does not seem to be a reflection of light, for I have more frequently seen it when the light has been behind the child or animal. I remember seeing it in a girl's eyes when I was in the light and she in a rather dark passage. She is now grown up; when I have an opportunity I will try to look for it again."

About a week ago I noticed this effect of light, very distinctly, in my youngest daughter's eyes. She was between some curtains, surrounded by shade, but the light shone from a lamp on to her face, and I was between her and the lamp. It was only by moving my head about carefully that every now and then the necessary point of vision was obtained from which the light in the eyes could be seen. The light was of an intensely bright red character. The experiment took place at tea-time and *eating* was going on, but I can hardly think in this case that it had much to do with it.

In looking through these letters from my former readers I came upon one from my friend Miss Jekyll, which reminded me that I had never said anything to Marco about a flower in my garden that I admire above measure for its delicate loveliness, namely *Ornithogalum nutans*, a bulb, of the "Star of Bethlehem" tribe. It throws up in the spring a fine strong stalk something after the manner of a wood hyacinth but with large greenish white flowers, the character and quality of which are quite, as far as I know, unique. It is very hardy. Mr. Robinson even cautioned me about it, telling me that it was apt to spread inconveniently, though at present I have not found it do so. Miss Jekyll writes of it: "Did you ever notice how much *Ornithogalum nutans* improves when gathered and placed in water? The flowers open and stand up and become much more delicate and satin-silvery."

"Satin-silvery" is a most happy expression as applied to this exquisite flower. I have been told that at Gatehampton, near Streatley, this plant has been found in quantities, wild, evidently an escape from some garden.

THE END

RICHARD CLAY AND SONS, LIMITED, LONDON AND BUNGAY.

www.ingramcontent.com/pod-product-compliance
Lightning Source LLC
Chambersburg PA
CBHW021037030726
47496CB00006B/1580